Recived from: B & B Freese

Belongs to Gloria Applegate

1-219-362-9067

TURN IT INTO GLORY

MEG WOODSON

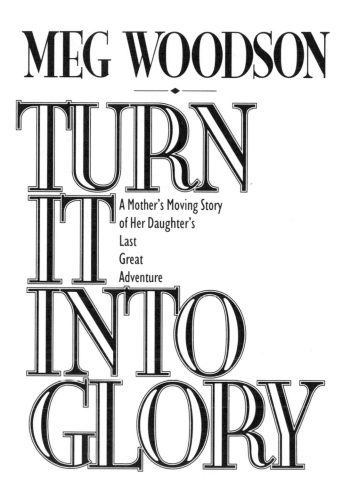

TURN IT INTO GLORY

A Mother's Moving Story
of Her Daughter's
Last
Great
Adventure

BETHANY HOUSE PUBLISHERS
MINNEAPOLIS, MINNESOTA 55438

"The Last Farewell," words by R. A. Webster for music written by
Roger Whittaker. © 1971 Tembo Music. © 1975 Arcola Music, Inc.
© Assigned 1975 to Croma Music Co. 130 West 57th St., NYC NY
10019.

Published by Bethany House Publishers
A Ministry of Bethany Fellowship, Inc.
6820 Auto Club Road, Minneapolis, Minnesota 55438

Published in association with the literary agency of Alive
Communications, Diamond Bar, California 91765.

Printed in the United States of America

Library of Congress Cataloging-in-Publication Data
Woodson, Meg
   Turn it into glory / Meg Woodson.
      p. cm.

    1. Cystic fibrosis—Patients—Ohio—Biography.
2. Mothers and daughters. I. Title.
RC858.C95W66   1991
362.1'9637'092—dc20
[B]   90–23734
ISBN 1–55661–178–1   CIP

To

Wendy Atkinson

and

Leo Zimmerman

They know what they meant to Peggie—
and to me.

With thanks to Benjamin G. Danis, Ph.D.,
who helped me *rewrite* my life
as well as my book.

MEG WOODSON is an award-winning writer/counselor known for her bestselling books, *If I Die at Thirty* and *Following Joey Home*. Having lost both her son and daughter to cystic fibrosis, she writes with a poignancy that defies description—a truly extraordinary wordsmith. Meg and her husband make their home in Cleveland, Ohio.

I first met Meg . . .

and Joe—

and Peggie Woodson—

on Thanksgiving Day, 1975. My husband and I were traveling back East to spend the holidays with my family, and since our route took us just south of Cleveland, Ohio, and since I was in the process of editing Meg's first book and was anxious to meet this gifted writer and her family face-to-face, we pulled in briefly to say hi. We ended up staying for their annual church-wide Thanksgiving dinner and beginning a professional friendship that has continued across time and distance. Whether face-to-face, or through Meg's eloquent words, the Woodsons are a family that, once met, can never be forgotten.

For those of you who have read Meg's other books, this will be like returning to sit beside an old friend. A friend who has lived through untold sorrows, and yet has endured and emerged on the other side.

For those of you who are new acquaintances—well, let me introduce you.

In many ways, Meg and Joe Woodson were very ordinary people. Joe was a pastor and Meg was a wife and mother. They lived in a middle-class suburb of Cleveland, Ohio, and had the requisite two children—one boy, one girl. But in every way that counts, Meg and Joe Woodson were extraordinary. They lived in Cleveland because both their children—Peggie and Joey—were born with cystic fibrosis and Cleveland had the best children's hospital specializing in that disease.

Joey, an endearing whirlwind of boyhood, died when he was twelve. Peggie, whom you will soon get to know, beat the odds—for a while.

In Meg's first book, *If I Die at Thirty*, her daughter Peggie dealt with the "why" questions of suffering as she faced not only the physical agony of cystic fibrosis, but also the emotional agony of her imminent mortality. Though she was just thirteen at that time, the answers she came up with satisfied her for the rest of her life. She never came back to those questions.

In Meg's second book, *Following Joey Home*, Meg herself dealt with the "why" questions, and while she admits she still rethinks them from time to time, it is never with any urgency.

This book, then, based on Peggie's final hospitalization, like John Gunther's *Death Be Not Proud* and the other classic elegies of literature, is Meg Woodson's final tribute to her daughter, Margaret Ann Woodson.

Though Meg and Joe would probably never admit this, it is also a tribute to them and to every other human spirit who has endured the unendurable.

Turn It Into Glory is outstanding in that, with her great writing skill and her unique maturity and insights, Meg deals with the profoundest questions humanity ever asks— the grief of a mother for a daughter, the unbearable weight of death in life, and the final life in death that is the believer's ultimate victory.

Above all, it is about abandoning oneself to divine providence, for *Turn It Into Glory* is not about the "whys" but about the "hows" of suffering. How did one particular family make it through their particular suffering? How did the young heroine more than make it—how did she make glory through it? Not, why wasn't God with them, but how was

He with them? How did they love each other? How did they not love each other? How did they live with the knowledge that they did not love each other enough? How did God love them and they Him?

Well, God loved them very much, which is, I suppose, why they never thought to ask, "Why is this happening to us—if God loves us?"

I urge you, read this book. While its sorrow may break your heart, its spiritual maturity will astound you, and the memory of its profound yet simple hope will return again and again to bear you up in the hard places of your own life. You will never regret one tear, and you will never forget Meg and Joe and Peggie Woodson.

Countless books have been written on grief and pain and suffering. Theologians have grappled, and will continue to grapple until we pass to a world where it no longer matters, with the ontological and the doctrinal and the theological. But when it comes right down to it, the real questions are the ones we ask in the darkness through our tears, and it often seems that the only comfort comes from those who will sit and listen and weep with us—sitting in the darkness, hoping for a glimmer of light. And that's what Meg Woodson offers.

Perhaps Philip Yancey, who has also known Meg for many years, sums it up best in his book *Disappointment with God:* "Meg's questions are questions of the heart, not the head. As a mother, she watched her children die slow, horrible deaths. Yet as a Christian she believes in God the loving Father. . . . Theological concepts don't amount to very much unless they can speak to someone like Meg Woodson, who gropes for God's love in a world bordered by grief."

Judith E. Markham

Prologue

I tugged the covers warm to my chin that Tuesday and snuggled into those early morning moments of contentment and security. No alarm ring.

But then Joe stuck his head in the bedroom door. "Peg phoned, Meg. She wants you to come. Room 420. She wants you to come now."

I lay unmoving for a spell, unheeding, and then alarm jangled every joint of my body and I sprang out of bed.

No. Oh, no. Please, God, no.

I could not think about it, but tore into my clothes. *Navy pants, and what top?* I jerked my vertically striped coverall top down over my head. How I hated being *round*, as Jan, my sculptor friend, saw it. Strangers analyzed you in all degrees of dress and undress when you lived in the hospital. I hadn't been *round* when I lived in with Joey during his last hospitalization.

Why was I thinking last *hospitalization?*

"Did Peggie say why she wanted me to come, Joe? Did she say if she wanted me to stay?"

"No, Meg, no. I asked what was wrong, but all she'd say was, 'Tell Mother to come. Tell Mother to come now.' "

I could not, not think about it, and I could tell from the

edge in Joe's voice how panicky he was too.

Peggie had been in the hospital for a week already and hadn't wanted me to come. I was used to it, used to the lengthy hospitalizations brought on by the increasing complications of her cystic fibrosis, and used to Peggie saying, "You hover when I'm sick, Mother. You worry. You make me feel like a little kid again."

Well, of course I worried—sometimes to the point of frenzy—but I did my best to cover it, to be available for Peg but not to impose my presence on her when she did not want it, which was often enough, even when presence and frenzy were not one.

I phoned the hospital as frequently as Peg's declarations of distance allowed, and a couple days ago I'd said, "I thought I'd drop by this afternoon."

And she'd said, putting puzzlement in her voice, *"Why?"* Peg had just turned twenty-three, but teenage *snottery* was still upon her.

Maybe I wasn't used to it. Not to the hurt of it.

I grabbed my red suitcase and threw in a nightgown, a book, changes of underwear. *Tell Mother to come. Tell Mother to come now.* I'd be in trouble when Peg saw the suitcase if what I read as a sign of disaster was not a sign, but, no—it was a portent.

Recalling how cold I'd gotten when I lived in with Joey and how scarce hospital pillows had been, I stuffed a plastic garbage bag with my furry robe, a quilt, both pillows from the bed, grabbed my purse, hugged Joe, promised to call the minute I knew what was going on, and raced for the car.

Oh, God, not Peggie. Not yet. I'm not ready. Please, please, God, not Peggie, too.

◇　　◇　　◇

I'm writing your hospital book, Peggie. I'm trying to write it perfectly for you, but I'm having a hard time writing it at all.

You always hated it when I had a hard time because of you. But I remember after Joey died, when I was wondering if he knew what was going on down here, how he could know and not feel bad when I felt so sad, and you said, "If Joey knows what's goin' on down here, God can fix it up so he can know and not feel bad." So I guess it's okay for me to tell you now that I'm not sure which is worse, reliving the times when we were as close as a mother and daughter could be or the times that left me without you in this forever-lonely world.

Most of the time there doesn't seem to be any point to doing anything but writing this book about you—keeping you alive and with me in the only way I know.

Did you know I have an office now? I rented it a few months after you died so I'd have to comb my hair in the mornings and go someplace. The blue-and-yellow rug New York Grandmother hooked for your college dorm room is hanging on one wall, and I bought a blue love seat and a large print of Monet's Water Lilies, *and I have a huge desk. Remember how I always needed more work space?*

I like it here, but a place can't take a person's place.

I wish you could be with me here in my office, Peggie. I wish you could be with me anywhere.

1

Some happenings you remember in every detail, always—as though nine years ago were this very morning. Nine years ago, though, it had been early, early morning. Four A.M. early. Cleveland dark and distorted in its emptiness. Joe driving like a crazy man.

Joey, our beloved twelve-year-old son Joey, lying so still in the back seat of the car, and then strangling for air, and then still. *Why so still?*

His cystic fibrosis had led him to pulmonary heart failure.

This is it, this is it, I'd told myself, my heart iced with terror, my heart stalling and shuddering with the car, and *knew* it was our last trip to the hospital with Joey. The doctor, when I'd wakened him from deep sleep, had not told me Joey would die. I'd had no experience that told me Joey would die. But I had a mother's instincts and my shuddering insides. Joey had died three weeks later.

Why did this trip to the east side of the city feel like that trip? No trip anywhere could feel like that trip. How could this trip be like that trip when just the Friday before last, Peg had slammed into the house bellowing, "Hi, Mother, your kid is home."

And soon she had been home in every corner of the house: pillowcases of dirty clothes lumped against the basement door, clean clothes hooked over the upstairs banister, plastic bags spilling medications over the living room couch, boxes of who-knew-what tripping you up in unsuspected spots.

When Peg was younger and still at home, I'd stalk through the house each night with a brown paper grocery bag collecting the gloves, the books, the Snoopy stationery—the *clutter*—she'd strewn from room to room throughout the day, and each night, with ritual, I'd dump it in her room.

But now, forget the mess. I enjoyed tripping over Peggie's who-knew-what.

Yet her paraphernalia didn't *fill* the house as much as Peg herself—five-foot-two, one hundred and twelve pounds of her, in brown cords and MASH T-shirt, brilliant blue knapsack on her back. She went nowhere without her fluorescent-blue knapsack.

Peggie *satisfied* the house with a lack of preciseness, with noise. Yes, her shoulders were rounded, and the upper half of her body heaved as she breathed, but the heaving was no worse than it had been for years . . . or was it? I couldn't remember. Maybe I didn't *want* to remember so much it was the same as *couldn't*.

Anyway, that was her body. Her spirit outdid her body. *If anybody can beat C.F., Peggie can.* Everybody said that. She carried no aura of death about her, this happy wayfarer.

I felt as though I came home again whenever Peg came home.

◇   ◇   ◇

"Jody spent last Friday night at my apartment, Mother. We had a riot," she had told me just the Friday before last as we settled down over Cokes at the kitchen table.

Peg had graduated from Bunting College in Bunting, Ohio, eight months before. She didn't have the strength to work full time, and nobody would hire her even part time with her C.F., but she had her insurance money and her apartment near the Bunting campus, and Jody and Shelley and Eric and Chuck.

"And John came down on Saturday, Mother, and we

really—" But then her face took on its defiant glare that said, *Some things are personal, Mother. Don't expect me to tell you everything.*

I didn't expect her to. It was enough for me to sit there with her at the kitchen table and have her tell me what she would, as we had sat there together so many times in the past with the sun flickering on her face through the red-checkered kitchen curtains. The eternal sun.

"Ya know, I think I'll go into the hospital when we get back from Peoria. Just once I'd like to go in before my lungs get really congested so it won't take so long to get them cleaned out."

Good. Oh, good. She always waited too long to go in.

"If they don't have a bed when we get back, I'll spend the night with Angie," she went on, glaring at me again, making sure I'd not expect her to spend the night with me. As though I hadn't figured out long ago that she drove the hour and a half from Bunting to Cleveland once a week to spend the night with Angie, her all-time-favorite nurse. "But what'll I say in Peoria, Mother? Come on, come on, what'll I say?"

We were going to Peoria, Illinois over the weekend to participate in a Cystic Fibrosis Awareness Day, each of us to conduct her own seminar. It would be Peg's first, a seminar for young adults with C.F.

"I brought a dress—if you can imagine—to wear for the banquet, the blue one with the lace, and I even brought a regular suitcase to pack it in, so I hope you're satisfied, Mother."

And then without any transition, without any foreboding on her part or mine that what she was about to tell me would alter the rest of her life, and mine, she said, "I have a quotation here I know you'll like. Pastor Arthur used it in his sermon last week, and I copied it down for you because I knew how much you'd like it."

She handed me a 3×5 card:

"Endurance is not just the ability to bear a hard thing, but to turn it into glory" (William Barclay).

"Isn't that neat? Pastor Arthur must have had a hard time that week, the way ministers do sometimes," she said, as only the daughter of a minister could, "because after he quoted that, he banged the pulpit with his fist and turned around and cried, and Pastor Arthur never does anything like that, *Ma.*"

Peggie usually called me "Mother." On rare occasions when she called me *Ma*, with hardness in her voice, it was her way of saying, "Now I'm not going to get emotional here, and you better not either, *Ma.*"

Joe and I had been soft sell in our children's spiritual nurturing. We taught them what we believed, and we tried to live out before them what we believed; but we knew their response had to be their own, and we left it to them.

Their response had been to follow where we led, almost without knowing they were following. Nothing moved me more readily to tears than the way Peg continued to pursue God, even now when she was out from under our influence—the way sailors of old pursued the sirens' call or poets longed for the west wind to sweep into their souls.

Endurance is not just the ability to bear a hard thing, but to turn it into glory.

And then, again without transition, Peg said, "Do you like my hair? I got a new perm."

I did like her hair, short curls in front, longer curls in back, their natural blond blending with the beige frames of the glasses we'd given her for her college graduation.

But Peggie more than liked her hair, her gold locks as essential to her as a miser's gold coins to him. She combed and fluffed and measured and critiqued those locks, *fingered and clinked and counted and stacked them*, ran compulsively to the nearest mirror to make sure they were still there.

"Father's going to get back from preaching out of town before we get back from our weekend, right, Mother?" she asked, and scribbled him a note, signing her name with a smile face after it, the smile face that had become as much a part of her signature as a smile was a part of her face.

Dear Fat-her,

Would you get the oil changed in my car if I pay?

Love, Peggie 😊

She'd thought up the *Fat-her* in her younger years and continued to use it—because her father hated it.

We flew to Chicago on Saturday morning and rented a car to drive to Peoria. Peg started out by driving ten miles the wrong way in Chicago traffic. "So? We saw downtown Chicago, didn't we? All we have to do is turn around and drive back. Is this an adventure or what?"

Her seminar participants gave her good ratings, and her spirits rode high as we drove back from Peoria on Sunday through endless cornfields. "I asked them what advantages came to them from their C.F., not disadvantages. It blew their minds."

A freakish April snowstorm blinded us as we approached O'Hare Airport, and we inched round and round in and out of the airport six times before we found the rent-a-car return lot.

"What a lark, Mother. I mean, all these adventures in one weekend. However, I would appreciate your making a list for me to turn in with the car. Put down: 1. no fluid in windshield wipers 2. wind blows in driver's door 3. right taillight out. And then in big letters write: WE COULD HAVE BEEN KILLED IN THE STORM."

Peg had low tolerance for inefficiency.

She kept sitting down to rest as we plodded through the airport terminal, gasping, coughing. I tried not to look, the same way I tried not to look when we shopped together, she finding the scarf or top she wanted, I standing in line to pay while she sat wherever she could find a place to sit . . . on a raised platform with the mannequins. With the unliving.

"There's an airport wheelchair over there, Peg, if you want to use it," I said, risking her wrath.

"I am not into wheelchairs, Mother. Never have been and am not now."

When we got home, she called the hospital, but they didn't have a bed. Sometimes you waited weeks for a bed.

Rumor had it that kids died waiting for beds, but then a bed opened up the next day, after Peg had spent the night with Angie.

One week ago. Could it be? I'd lived a lifetime since 7:20 this morning. I'd be ancient, shrunken and senile before I finished this trip across Cleveland.

Peggie had not kissed me hello when she came home last weekend, nor hugged me good-bye, nor said *I love you* in between.

"I am not into mush, Mother. Don't clutch."

I had clutched for a while after Joey's death, but I didn't anymore, as far as I knew. Lots of parents of healthy children were more possessive than I. Yes, Joe hugged Peg to him against her will, but was it fair that I get the flack from that? Was it fair that she complain about our prying or our demands on her when what she was really complaining about was her inability to free herself from her final dependence on us? No, it was not fair.

Still, she was more fair than she had been in adolescence. How I'd prayed that Peg wouldn't die in adolescence, her shouts of disdain frozen forever in my ears. But we'd become friends again *once she'd established herself*, as she put it. Still with tension between us, but friends.

And she had called for me this morning. She always called for me when her need called for someone who would sacrifice for her, and she was there for me in my need, too, though not in like degree or with like demeanor.

And we did have that last wonderful weekend together. Now why was I thinking *last* weekend? *Last* hospitalization? *Please, God, not the last of Peggie too.*

No, Peg didn't say "I love you." Peg didn't let me say "I love you," but she knew I did, though not how much. No mode of measure existed that could weigh my love for her. I barely let myself know how much I loved Peggie.

◊   ◊   ◊

And then suddenly I was in the hospital elevator, Snoopy dancing on top of a piano on one wall. I passed Mary, the head nurse, as I sped down the fourth floor. Mary was strong and beautiful in body and spirit, and everyone respected and loved her.

"Good to see you, Mrs. Woodson," she said. Not, "What are you doing here at 8:30 in the morning, Mrs. Woodson?" She glanced at my suitcase, but not in surprise, and it was a second sign to me. Though small compared to the portent of Peg's phoning me to come, it slowed my steps.

And then I stood in the doorway of room 420, raincoat hanging open because it wouldn't quite close, shoulder bag dangling from the crook of my left arm, the arm holding the bulging garbage bag. My right arm held the suitcase. *If only it weren't so bright a red.*

Inside the room in the first bed to the left lay a blond girl, but her hair was straight and her body long. Not Peggie. In the first bed to the right lay a black girl. Not Peggie. On the right on the far side of the room a pixie of a thing with dark hair waving to her waist sat on the edge of her bed, legs dangling, arms pressed around a woman who stood facing her, the woman's arms enveloping her. Definitely not Peggie.

At the foot of the bed on the far left of the room stood a wheelchair with an oxygen tank strapped to the back. But Peg had only been on oxygen twice in her life, once at sixteen when her left lung collapsed and once intermittently during therapy to help her cough. I checked the number over the door again. 420—and it was only a four-bed ward.

I forced my eyes to move to the form in the fourth bed, and it was slight, and its blond hair was curly, and its face, turned toward me, was Peggie's face with oxygen tubes in its nose. And its eyes, locked into mine, were Peggie's enormous, gorgeous, courageous-blue eyes.

I stood shock-still and stared, mouth hung wide by horror, clammy from head to toe.

But then I closed my mouth—she must not see my horror—and walked as in a trance toward her.

"Hi, *Ma,*" she said.

"Hi, honey."

"John's coming tonight," she said.

"I'll get lost."

"Good." She giggled. "And guess what? Angie's my nurse this afternoon."

I looked casually down to my sides. "I brought a few things with me in case you wanted me to stay."

"I'll ask Mary to get you a cot, *Ma*," she said.

And all my inner organs shook. All my vital organs shuddered with terror. And I *knew*—yet didn't know.

2

I didn't put my bag or baggage down but stood before Peggie like a giant scale, weighed down first on one side and then the other, while she told me about the occupants of the room—an old-time scale with a woman's face, smile molded into gray metal.

"That's Mandy, and she has cystic fibrosis," Peg said, pointing to the fairy creature of the long black tresses, "and that's her mother, Mrs. Canfield. I've been in with them before, and they're fantastic. And that's Karol," she added, pointing to the black girl. "She has sickle-cell anemia and something else besides, and she throws up all the time, and we don't bother her because she's too sick to be bothered.

"And that's Roseanne Kovach," she concluded, waving disdainfully toward the tall, blond girl. "She had cancer, but she doesn't anymore, and she doesn't need to be here. She just doesn't want to go to school."

I soon discovered for myself how fantastic Mrs. Canfield was, how much she'd fetched and carried for Peg and wheelchaired her about the past few days. And it seemed that Peg was right about Roseanne too, for she was hardly ever in the room, her main purpose in hospitalization being to avoid phone calls from Sister Mary Margaret.

Roseanne and Peg shared a phone, and three times that day I answered it when it was Roseanne's school calling.

"I'm sorry, but Roseanne Kovach isn't here right now, Sister Mary Margaret."

"I think Roseanne Kovach is with the doctor just now, Sister Mary Margaret."

"No, Sister Mary Margaret, I have no idea where Roseanne is."

I could have gone looking for her, but it eased my tension to defy authority of any kind.

After Peg's introductions that morning, a therapist came in to pound the mucus loose and hopefully out of her lungs, much as you pound a catsup bottle to make the catsup run out, and I found a lawn chair—the resident version of a visitor's chair—and sat in it, my coat wrapped around me protectively. Peg was not going to comment on the reason for her call, and I did not need to ask.

Patients in the hospital were wakened early for one reason or another but went back to sleep, so the scene was drowsy now, the colors muted, though I could make out the red-and-green crocheted afghan on Mrs. Canfield's cot under the window next to Mandy's bed, and Mandy's yellow-kitten quilt. Roseanne was snoozing under a blanket covered with what I assumed was her astrological sign, and Peggie's pink butterfly sheet lay folded at the foot of her bed ready to be used as a spread when her bed was made up for the day.

The room didn't have an institutional air. Yes, the beds were brown Formica, as were the bed trays and cabinets, but the big windows across from Mandy's and Peggie's beds had yellow and orange and blue draw drapes, closed now, and the small windows lining the wall facing the nurses' station were curtained to match the drapes. Homey.

Peggie always said that no hospital in the world compared with Rainbow Babies and Children's Hospital, and, no, she didn't mind being an adult on the adolescent floor as long as they didn't take her away from Dr. Rathburn.

How many weeks all-told had we lived in this hospital? And why did we live more intensely here than we lived anywhere else?

For years I'd had nightmares, night after night, in

which, for what seemed like all night, I tried to find my way home—and couldn't. But spent hour after hour huddled in the New York City subway system, lost, and then hour after hysterical hour boarding wrong bus after wrong bus trying to find the house in Queens in which I'd grown up.

Only when I finally walked in the door of Rainbow Babies and Children's Hospital in Cleveland, Ohio, did the nightmares end—only my unshuttered, yet sheltered dream mind able to admit that in some black-humorless way this *death-house* was not only homey, but home.

I yanked my raincoat angrily around me and bumped my lawn chair back till it hit the wall hard. I did not like feeling such belonging in such a place.

◇   ◇   ◇

Do you remember when I found your pink butterfly sheet for you, Peg? You were in the hospital, and I trudged in and out of every sheet-selling store in the Parmatown Mall, calling you up to describe every Peggie-like sheet I could find . . . a rainbow sheet, a Woodstock sheet. . . . None would do till I called from The May Company and described the butterfly sheet. "Yes, Peggie, I know you think pink is a sweet color, but it isn't really pink, more of a dusky rose, with yellow butterflies and puffs of white clouds against a blue sky. . . . No, Peggie, you don't have to keep it if you don't like it."

But it had been love at first sight between you and the butterfly sheet, and from then on you never went to the hospital without your covering that said, I am a butterfly person. Even now, I am me. Even here, I am home.

I never told you how much the sheet cost. More than we could afford.

We had you buried under that sheet. People who knew how managerial you'd been were shocked that you didn't leave instructions for your funeral, but you never gave your funeral a thought. So we tried to plan it the way you would have liked it and made the funeral director tuck you round with the butterfly sheet. I knew you'd hate to be covered with satin and ruffles and hate too, to be wearing a Sunday dress, so you wore your navy cords and the red blouse with the white collar we found in the big sale at The Gap—with your hair all clean and fluffy, and with a spray of yellow mums on the top of the casket from your father and me. I was going to have a smile face pasted on each mum, but the funeral director suggested that one smile face in the middle of the arrangement would have a stronger, yet subtle effect. He saved me from asininity.

Oh, Peggie, we made mistakes with you all our lives, but we always tried our best.

Not once since your death, Peggie, have I raced through the night trying to find my way home.

It is all right now, isn't it, Peggie, for me to say I love you!

3

I felt better after the room woke up.

Now that the drapes were open and the lights on and I could see the bed coverings clearly, together with the get-well cards and rock star posters taped to the walls, what color!

And commotion! With Peggie and Mandy sign-languaging across the room to each other, and nurses and doctors and technicians scurrying in and out, and Roseanne slinking in and out, and poor Karol throwing up. Neatness and hush and white were not the order of the day.

And I felt better after my cot arrived.

I remembered where they kept the sheets and made the cot up under the window next to Peggie's bed, with my suitcase tucked underneath and my book and toilet kit on the window sill. I wished it all didn't seem like a repeat performance, but at least I had *my place to be.*

The best thing was that Peggie felt better as the day progressed, off oxygen, walking to the bathroom and down the hall to the treatment room to wash her hair in the sink that lent itself to the most efficient hair-washing, and to condition her hair, and to air-dry her hair. No way would she lay her head back on her pillow till the air had dried every hair.

"You do know, don't you, Mother, that C.F. patients often get worse before they get better when they come in the hospital? The antibiotics loosen up the mucus in your lungs, and you feel lousy before you get it all up."

"Yes, honey, I know that."

"And I am only on oxygen at night. I mean, it's on my wheelchair just in case I need it when I go out."

I let her have it. Of course I let her have hope. She might have made me doubt my lack of hope had not the bad signs outweighed the good.

Like the time I was over talking to Mandy and Mrs. Canfield, and Peggie went into a coughing fit. I kept on talking to the Canfields, Peg having trained me through the years to act as though nothing of consequence was happening when she coughed.

But when I wandered back to her, "Where were you?" she hissed. "Why do you think I asked you here?"

It became apparent as the day progressed that she had asked me there, in part, to stand beside her when she coughed—not to do anything for her, just to stand beside her. Her old coughing fits had been racking, but these new coughing fits were a new thing, so rampant that once she started coughing, I think she was afraid she'd not stop, not be able to breathe again.

I could not pull for air alongside her and not be deathly afraid too.

And then Dr. Rathburn made rounds, and I followed him out of the room.

"What did you ask him, and what did he say?" Peg demanded when I came back into the room.

"What happened, and I don't know."

She laughed, Dr. Rathburn was known for his cryptic comments to parents. I didn't tell her that I had also asked, "Is she going to get better?" And that he had said "I don't know" to that too, his not knowing an enormous sign because I'd asked him that naked question many times before, and he had never given me that outrageous answer.

After that I tracked Dr. Rathburn down while I was out and about on other business so Peggie wouldn't see me and ask what he said.

◇   ◇   ◇

Joe came that afternoon, and I felt so much better with him there, though I didn't share my *knowing* with him.

It was a little joke in our church that no matter how many times Peg went into the hospital during a year, no matter how sick she was, Joe announced it to the congregation by saying, "Peggie is in Rainbow Babies and Children's Hospital for her annual routine clean-out."

"How is she really?" people asked me afterward.

Joe loved his only daughter so much that he had never been able to acknowledge how sick she was.

"I'm sorry I didn't get it done before, Peg," he told her that afternoon, "but I had the oil in your car changed today and filled your gas tank. I put it on my charge."

"Can the man be telling me I don't have to pay?"

"No, Peggie, you don't have to pay," he said with the softness in his voice I heard only when he was giving of himself to Peggie. Later he left to go to our church's Tuesday Night Discussion Group. I was glad his work kept him from spending all his time at the hospital. He could not have endured.

I replaced my raincoat with my long fleecy robe belted at the waist. It was warmer than my coat, and for the next six weeks I lived in Peggie's room and traveled up and down the hall feeling like an overstuffed blue pillow, tufted in the middle.

I told myself that this was no time to be concerned with the way I looked. But I told myself too that another *round* person would understand how much more able I would have felt to face the immediate future, and the future beyond, which seemed no future, had I not been *round* but *regular.*

Peggie didn't have a temperature. The doctor couldn't explain why she stayed so hot, why she needed the room so cold. He hadn't been able to explain it for Joey either.

When John came that first evening, I *got lost* by crawling into my cot, robe and all, and pulling the quilt over my head. John sat on Peggie's bed and they talked in low tones that lulled me into half-sleep in which I half-dreamed . . . of Peggie in the hospital . . . in days past. . . .

◇   ◇   ◇

I kept telling the doctor I was in labor, but the pains were not regular, and the doctor kept telling me that unless the pains were regular, it was false labor. I still had the scraps of paper on which for two days and nights I kept track of the pains. *3 min. 8 min. 1 min. 10 min.*

He was right. The pains weren't regular. The doctor just didn't know yet that Peggie Woodson didn't do anything in regular fashion.

I didn't know it yet myself, just that we had tried for four years to have this baby, and that it was only after we'd been advised to adopt that I'd become pregnant. By then I'd told the world so many times, "This time I know I'm pregnant," no one believed me when I was, and now our baby was about to be born and the doctor would not believe me.

When, after an eternity of pain etched forever on my pelvic parts, I called him again and said, *"I am having a baby,"* he agreed to take a look. And I, indeed having a baby and determined to carry it off with decorum when the great and final moment arrived, forgot decorum, and shrieked, "Help!"

It was against regulations, but they let me take her home when she weighed four pounds, thirteen ounces. I wasn't sure I wanted to. Oh, she was a wondrous creature, beyond my dreams, but slippery. And yet she could stiffen her body as stiff as could be. I held her squalling-stiff on my lap just before we left the hospital. "Give me a handbook, please," I shouted to the doctor. "I can't go home without one."

◇   ◇   ◇

She never acted quite right. "She takes one bottle after another," I told the doctor, "but she doesn't gain, and she wheezes all the time." The protectiveness I felt toward this moist lump of snuggling humanity stunned me.

"A lot of babies are slow gainers, Mrs. Woodson," the doctor said. "All babies wheeze."

As time moved on, however, the indications that my

baby was flawed—in some minor, fixable way, of course—became too obvious to be ignored, and I called the doctor yet again, holding Peg close to the phone so he could hear her wheeze.

"Look, she's six months old, you've changed her formula seven times, and she weighs ten pounds. I sit up half the night giving her one bottle after another. They play 'The Star Spangled Banner,' the TV screen goes blank, and she throws the whole mess up and screams for more."

"I didn't know she wheezed like that," the doctor said, and agreed to take a look.

And when I brought her in, he said, "There's a screening test for a disease called cystic fibrosis, Mrs. Woodson. It affects the glands of the body, including the sweat glands. I'm going to press Peg's thumb on this gel. If her sweat has a high salt content, a symptom of cystic fibrosis, the gel will change color."

Then, when he'd done it, he went into the next room, and I heard him say to the nurse, "I think we've got one."

"Will you spell the name of that disease?" I asked, and wrote it down, and said it over and over to myself on the way home so I wouldn't forget it. *Cystic fibrosis. Cystic fibrosis.*

I think we've got one. I didn't worry about forgetting that.

I took Peg into the hospital the next day for a definitive test. They tied her up in a plastic bag and waited for enough sweat to drip off her to analyze. We lived in Jackson, Tennessee, a fairly small town, and were fortunate to have a pediatrician who tested for cystic fibrosis, however primitive his methods.

"A friend gave me a pamphlet on cystic fibrosis," I told him. "It says that no baby born with C.F. has outlived childhood. Is that true?"

"They make those pamphlets to raise money. They put the worst side of the disease forward."

"Has any baby with C.F. outlived childhood?"

"You're jumping the gun. Let's wait for the results of the test."

So—it was true. I wore self-control like a breastplate,

the only armor I could find for my tender mother's breast.

"Give me your medical books, please."

I was pathologically nonassertive in those days, but some things can't wait if you're a mother. Like your baby being born. Like finding out if your baby is going to die.

The doctor gave me his medical books, and I read everything I could find on cystic fibrosis, and the best I could find was one mention of one boy who lived to be twelve.

"One out of every two thousand Caucasian babies born in this country is born with C.F., Joe, but the books say that only one has lived to be twelve."

Joe agreed with the doctor in that he could have waited to talk about these things.

The next day I was crawling into bed for a nap when the doctor came to talk. "You can take your nap later, Mrs. Woodson."

Many times in the years since, I've thought, *Haven't had that nap yet.*

"As I've explained, Mrs. Woodson, cystic fibrosis is a glandular disease. You'll add salt to Peggie's food in hot weather; that will take care of the sweat glands. The digestive glands in the pancreas and intestines are also involved; you'll give Peggie pancreatic enzymes whenever she eats that will aid in her absorption of food."

The doctor spoke in a flat voice as though he were quoting his medical books, as though he didn't care about Peggie. Or else as though he were protecting himself from his caring. He was a nice doctor.

"The glands in the lungs, instead of producing a thin, slippery mucus that acts as a cleansing agent for the lungs, produce a thick, sticky mucus that acts as fly paper for bacteria. Peggie will have chronic, low-grade respiratory infections, but she'll take antibiotics routinely to hold it down."

The doctor also said, when I pressed, that while antibiotics could hold down respiratory infection, they could not eliminate it, nor could anything prevent the destructive scarring—fibrosis—of the lungs caused by the viscous mucus.

And, "Yes, yes, Mrs. Woodson, most babies born with cystic fibrosis die of respiratory failure." And, "No, no, no, Mrs. Woodson, to my knowledge no baby born with cystic fibrosis has outlived childhood."

Judgment Day. It was the great and final day of judgment, and God said, "Cast this woman into outer darkness." And still I could not weep or wail or gnash my teeth.

◊   ◊   ◊

You continued to eat a lot, Peggie, but you did gain on your new regimen. We weighed you in a box tied to the top of a peanut scale, till, finally . . . you weren't peanuts anymore. And for the next year, taking tetracycline every day, you didn't have one respiratory infection.

And you smiled a lot and laughed clear-as-a-gurgling-brook when we played peek-a-boo or when you splatted your dinner over half the kitchen floor.

And you would not go to sleep without your "night-night."

We'd hand you a bottle of formula.

Wham! On the floor!

Orange juice? Rattle? Teether? Teddy?

Wham! Bang! Scream!

I was proud of the way you knew what you wanted and went after it—at least after I knew it was your raggedy blue blanket you wanted.

Your father and I fought over who would push your buggy, and the doctor said he could tell from looking at you that we'd "got a bright one." He had a knack for knowing what we'd got one of.

I can still feel your arms wrapped around my neck when we went out in the yard at night and looked up at the stars, and I sang low in my dreadful monotone, "God's friendly night. God's friendly night. I love God's friendly night."

Oh, Peggie, know, Peggie, that those were celestial days.

◊   ◊   ◊

As her health improved and the consumingness of our worry abated, we longed for another love-joy child, a healthy child to guarantee the continuance of the greatest love and joy we had known.

"Go ahead," the doctor said. "C.F. is caused by a recessive gene. Every time you have a baby, you have a three-out-of-four chance of having a healthy baby. The odds are with you."

We took the chance. We lost. Though cooing, contented, beloved-son Joey, born two years after Peggie, was such a winner, we didn't think of ourselves as losers.

I didn't need a doctor to tell me Joey had C.F. Every time I kissed him and tasted the salt in his sweat, I *knew* those kisses were kisses of death.

We took both children to the leading children's hospital in our area of the country, Le Bonheur in Memphis, to make sure we were doing everything for them that could be done, and the leading pediatrician in the Midsouth said, "Cystic fibrosis comes in all degrees of severity. With your children . . . well, take your children home and enjoy them while you have them."

The weather on our trip home was frigid, and our car heater was broken. Joey lay in his tiny car bed in the back seat all wrapped up in blankets, Peggie sitting beside him, the miniature mother, all wrapped up in blankets. I folded into myself in the front seat.

They were both going to die, my Peggie and my Joey. They were both going to get pneumonia and die before we ever got them home.

I was folded into myself now under the quilt on my cot in room 420 in Rainbow Babies and Children's Hospital as Peg's and John's voices droned on, folded up tight against the frigid temperature of the room, against all frigid feelings. I did not want to think about trips home from the hospital because that made me think about last trips home from the hospital, and last trips home I could not think about.

If only I could have followed the doctor's advice, accepted the fact that my children were going to die, and spent the time I had with them in enjoyment of them, but— I could not.

34

We lived in the kitchen of the parsonage all winter back then. We couldn't afford to heat the rest of the house, and it was a big kitchen with a wicker couch and rocker. I can still see Peggie toddling around that back room in her red Buster Brown pants and red-and-white striped top, still with just a little blond fuzz on her head, and I can still hear her asking, "What-a-matta, Mama? What-a-matta?" I see many pictures of Peggie in those early days. Climbing onto her first swing under the pecan tree in our backyard and falling off backwards, climbing on again and falling off frontwards, climbing on again. Peggie and Joey standing side by side in the Cherub Choir in church, big red bows under their chins, unself-conscious Joey twisting his white robe over his head, but Peg solemnly singing out her "Jesus Loves Me" so everyone would know.

I see Peggie in endless poses from those days, but the only thing I hear her say is, "What-a-matta, Mama?"

◇　◇　◇

We flew to Columbia Presbyterian Medical Center in New York City then. They first identified C.F. as a disease, and we came home with mist tents and air compressors and slant boards and instructions to give each child an aerosol and a half hour of therapy four times a day, but we didn't come home with hope.

Peggie was so wanting of me back then, her little-girl body blending or bulldozing into mine whenever *she* could hold *me* still. But I was busy back then, fixing aerosols, holding aerosols to faces, doing therapy, sterilizing mist tents, mixing enzymes in applesauce. I pushed Peggie away back then. In a frenzy to keep Peggie with me, I pushed her away from me.

◇　◇　◇

How I wish I could do motherhood over, Peg—have you back, little. Oh, big, too, but I suspect that my worry damaged you most when you were little, gave the twig an anxious, guilty bent.

I'd cry a lot more if I had you back, I can tell you that,

35

*and be a lot less busy. Oh, I'd not cry so you'd see, but
enough so that my anxiety over you children wouldn't build
inside me till I couldn't sleep at night, and I'd yell at you
for no reason and my depression blighted your lives.*

*When I need to trigger tears now, I think back to some-
thing Joey used to say when I had a playful moment: "Hey,
look, Peggie, Mama's in a good mood!" If anything's going
to trigger tears, that "Mama's in a good mood" will do it,
because Joey always said it with surprise.*

◇   ◇   ◇

And then we heard about the C.F. Center in Cleveland—
this very center in which I now lie on this very cot—heard
that they rarely lost a patient here at any age. And we roared
up from Tennessee, and they were pioneering here, and the
doctor said—we clearly heard the doctor say—that with
early diagnosis and intensive preventive treatment, C.F. patients could live into middle adulthood. And we packed up
lock, stock, and medical equipment and moved to Cleveland.

I must have fallen all the way asleep then, because for
the second time that day the ringing of the phone woke me.
John said it was for me, and I disentangled myself from my
cot and walked past John and Peg, robe trailing.

"Pay me no mind," I said, and they giggled.

It was Becky's mother—Becky being Peg's best church
friend—calling after Discussion Group.

"What's up, Meg? Joe said Peggie was in the hospital
and that things didn't look good. And he was mumbling
about oil in her car, and what was free oil in her car when
he'd freely give his life to save her."

"Yes," I said, conscious of listening ears, and crawled
back into my cot, quilt over my head, and cried. It was too
much. If I cried so hard I never stopped, let it be. If I fell
apart into so many pieces I could never put myself back
together, just let it be.

Joe said things didn't look good. How could it be?

*Oh, God, help Joe, and help me cry all the tears I've held
in for so many years, for Joe, for Joey, for Peggie, for me, for*

36

all children everywhere alive with, and dead from, this cursed disease, and for their families.

After a while I heard John leave and I looked over at Peg. She'd been sitting up, animated, as long as he was there, but now she collapsed on her bed, fumbling for her oxygen. And I, though lying flat already, collapsed on mine.

Help! I shrieked in the hollow of my head. *Oh, God, help! Give me a handbook, please. I can't do this without one.*

4

*A*nd then the dark of night was upon us, and three times in the wee hours nurses shook me awake. "Peggie wants you, Mrs. Woodson."

And I struggled up and sat by Peg's side as she told me her fears. This fearless child of mine rambled on through the night about her fears, and I cannot remember one of them, but I remember how they overcame her, because I remember how this touch-me-not child of mine said, "Put your hand on my leg, Mother." "Mother, touch my hand."

The danger signs that had begun at 7:20 that morning flashed in my head like neon lights, on and off, through the night hours. Peg's fears overcame me too.

It was not in any way a restful night, for the bathroom was in the corner between Peggie's bed and my cot, so in addition to being wakened by shaking, I was wakened by the *tramp-tramp* of feet past my bed, door sliding open, light in my eyes, door sliding closed, *chug-whoosh*.

My place to be sat on a major thoroughfare. I knew that no one was trying to harass me, but, still, I wanted to slam open a window, stick my head out, and yell, "Somebody's trying to sleep in here."

And worse than the noise was the lack of privacy. Sleeping is a private thing, especially for a private person like me. I could not sleep on the edge of Main Street. And I had to sleep. How could I take care of Peggie if I couldn't sleep?

When finally I dozed and woke on my own, and sat up in my bed, I saw by the dawn's dove-gray light that Peg was also sitting up in hers.

"About time, Mother," she snapped.

But I knew I hadn't overslept because the drapes were still drawn and all the familiar shapes in the room hid behind the shadowy contours of sleep.

Two large machines that hadn't been there last time I looked stood by Peggie's bed, one at the foot and one at the head: an oxygen cannula led to her nose from the left; an intravenous tube came from the right dripping antibiotics into her broviac, the I.V. hook-up permanently implanted in her chest.

"Hey, *Ma*," she whispered. "You remember that quotation?"

"About turning hard times into glory?" I whispered back, a sinking within.

"Yeah." The word wisped its way to me through the dimness and the silence.

And Peg looked around meaningfully at the tubes, at the cold metal boxes, and her face lit up like a roaring bonfire, her head nodding, flames leaping up and down.

And I nodded back at her. I did, and it was the end of the signs for me. Not that they didn't keep coming, more clearly, more quickly, but I didn't notice them as signs anymore because I *knew* where the signs were pointing. The quotation had been given to Peggie to guide her on her last, great adventure.

Oh, God. Oh, God.

Some few happenings you remember in every detail, always—as though another world, another time, were this very age, this earth. I will remember in every detail, always, Peggie as she looked that morning propped up on her pillows—rumpled, wan, and aglow with wonder.

And I was glad she snapped "about time" at me first, because it meant she was no plastic saint, her put-downs of her mother as native to her being as her piety. Though the strength of the resolution she made in the weak light of that morning was evidenced by the fact that in the strained weeks to come, all the mornings and nights in which she lived through her dying, Peggie hardly snapped at me at all.

It was the end of the signs and the beginning of the glory.

5

I *don't think you knew, that fateful morning, that you were going to die, Peg, just that a harder time was coming than you had ever known. Peggie Woodson would not give up without a ripsnorter.*

You had terrible times in the next six weeks, but let the good times roll *was your philosophy, and* let the glory shine on good and bad.

You worried to the end about whether or not you were "making the glory," so in case you still aren't aware of all the ways you turned all your hospital times into glory, I want to tell you now.

1. You were the best patient you were capable of being. You were not the best possible patient, but you were the best it was possible for you to be.

2. You bore what appeared to you to be the ineptitude of a select few around you without sounding off at the inept.

3. You bore with class everything crass disease and medical science imposed on your body.

4. You loved your friends more than you loved yourself.

5. You made the uttermost effort to leave your father and me with good memories.

6. You had no fear of death, though you were scared half to death of everything else.

7. You never asked God Why? *or railed against Him, but recognized Him as He acted in your behalf at every turn.*

8. *And until your body robbed your spirit of options, you opted for joy. You* **Peggie'd** *everyone you came in contact with.*

I have three major regrets about my mothering of you, Peggie: that I didn't laugh with you more; that I didn't spend more time with you; and that I didn't tell you how proud I was of you while I still had a chance to tell you, while you still needed to hear it with all your approval-hungry soul.

I was so proud of the way you handled your life, Peggie, in and out of the hospital, your life and your death. No mother was ever more proud of a daughter than I of you.

6

I was wide awake, then, early that morning of my first full day in the hospital. God knew where Peggie was and He knew where she was going—had prepared her for her journey before she knew where she was going. But, oh, the journey's end. . . . I cracked the shade beside my cot and waited for the day to become as stirred up as I. Who could sleep?

Well, Peggie could sleep and all the other C.F.ers on the floor. They got more lively as the day progressed, till midnight was party time, but early morning was can't-wake-up time, and not even Peg's rapture at the prospect of *glorifin'* kept her awake.

Sandy, Peggie's nurse for the day shift, hooked up an I.V. in a wholly unconscious Peggie, flushed it out, and unhooked it. Breakfast trays clanged in while Peggie and Mandy still nested in their beds, barely the tip of a baby bird head peeking out of each.

It really was Peg in that bed, though, and I really was here, and Peggie really was going to die. My baby Peg, my toddler Peg, my schoolgirl . . .

◊   ◊   ◊

I'm just letting myself think of your girlhood, Peg. A remembered joy is a stabbing pain the first time you remember it, and your elementary school years were a joy to

*me. You could do a lot for yourself in those years, and yet
. . . you needed me.*

*Confided in me, your bony body pressed into mine as
you sat by my side on the couch. "At recess what I usually
do, Mother, is run for a swing before they're all taken. Swing-
ing is something you can do by yourself. You know how it
is, Mother, if you can't play the running games—or if you
don't have a friend."*

*A remembered pain is a stabbing pain the first time you
remember it. Remembering your loneliness stabs at the un-
protected parts of me, Peg, because I suspect that you picked
up on my loneliness, that if I hadn't been lonely, you might
not have been lonely either.*

*Still, your elementary school days were basically a joy
for you as well as for me. You compensated for lack of pop-
ularity by excelling in your studies. "The teacher set up an
honors table today, Mother, and guess whose name was the
first one she called? Peggie Woodson! My name!"*

*And you had your stamp collection and your shell col-
lection and your book collection. What was it, Peg, two
hundred and forty books in your library, indexed in strict
accord with the Dewey Decimal System?*

*And when you were in the sixth grade and we asked God
very specially, remember how He gave you Heidi for a
friend?*

*Remember the vacation at the end of the sixth grade
when we walked from New York Grandmother's house to
Woolworths and bought the box of fifty Crayola crayons and
the jumbo "Jumbo the Elephant" coloring book? I can still
hear you hooting, "Isn't this the dumbest thing you ever
heard of, Mother?"*

*Then we sat in the backyard under the maple tree and
bumped elbows as we each colored a page on our side of the
book.*

*"You stay inside the lines pretty good for someone your
age, Mother."*

*"Well, I'd do better, but I'm trying not to make you look
bad, Peggie."*

You laughed up at me with eyes that seemed even bigger

and bluer than they do now, perhaps because you wore your hair so short back then. Remember how much it meant to you that your yellow hair curled up the slightest bit at the ends? I commented on that a lot to you, Peggie, but never on your stick-like arms sticking out of your tops, stick-like legs sticking out of your shorts.

Thinking about the coloring-book vacation brings back such feelings of companionship, Peg. Perhaps because it was your last fling with childhood. Perhaps because we both sensed that we would not know that kind of companionship again.

◊   ◊   ◊

Only two nurses who had been on the floor when I lived in with Joey were still there, but Mrs. Abrams, the therapist that morning, had been there not only nine, but twenty years ago, had taught Joe and me to do therapy on our first trip to Cleveland.

"You didn't do all the positions, *old friend*," I said to her now, not in condemnation but inquiry, as I walked her to the door. "And you didn't lower the head of the bed when you did the lower lobes."

"Peg can't breathe with her head down, Mrs. Woodson," Mrs. Abrams said kindly. "She can't hold up for a whole therapy."

When had this happened?

Suddenly the hyper-energy drained out of me. The all-but-sleepless night, the shock of yesterday—everything caught up with me. Two things inevitably pushed me over the edge when I was on the edge of giving way—unkindness, and kindness.

The first thing Peg did at ten-thirty or so when the room roused itself was to turn off her oxygen and wash her hair. No, she didn't want my help, thank you. She could carry her own shampoo and her own conditioner and her own final rinse. She was capable of finding a towel. But I noticed that while yesterday she'd walked down the hall to the much-lauded sink in the treatment room, today she walked only to the sink in the far corner of her own room.

Such a little thing, yet as she walked the few yards across the room, I felt her disappear over a far horizon.

"Would you see what T-shirts I have left in my drawer, Mother, and ask Mandy which one she wants me to wear today?"

"Ask Mandy?"

"Mandy picks out my T-shirt every morning. Come on, Mother. It gives her something to do, and she likes doing it."

"Well, what'll it be today, Mandy," I said. "The panda T-shirt, the Let's Conquer C.F. T-shirt, or the red football T-shirt?"

Mandy's face blossomed into a sweet-joyous smile. "The panda T-shirt," she cried, clapping her hands, and Peg would wear no other. It was Peg's favorite, too, a gift from Dr. Rathburn during an earlier hospitalization when he'd come back from a medical conference in Washington, D.C., and a side trip to the Washington zoo.

So Peggie wore her light blue cords and her light-blue T-shirt with the panda on the front. It made her look less like a patient, all that pretty blue and her clean blond hair. I was glad the hospital encouraged patients to dress in everyday clothes. It made them feel less like patients.

That morning, though, the mechanics of getting ready for the day exhausted Peg, and she went back into the bed Sandy had made while she was out of it, pink butterfly sheet on top, and back on her oxygen.

"You don't have to worry about a thing when Sandy's your nurse, Mother."

I could tell that already, Sandy's competence was matched only by her compassion. And she was pretty, too, titian hair shimmering about her piquant face like the light of a rising sun.

"And this afternoon Angie's coming back. Boy, Sandy and Angie in one day. *And*," she added in conspiratorial tones, "Roseanne Kovach is going home today. Yah-yah! *And* Joanne Avellone's coming into Roseanne's bed. I've been in with Joanne before, and she's great.

"Ya know, Mother, you simply have not been around the

hospital enough to understand what an exceptional room this is. I mean, four really great patients, and Karol's mother being a nurse, and Mrs. Canfield being Mrs. Canfield. You should appreciate this room more, Mother."

I lost count of the times Peggie upbraided me in the next six weeks for not properly appreciating the room.

"Now you tell me, Mother, was I right about the T-shirt or what? Did you see Mandy's face light up? Just look over there at her and Mrs. Canfield."

I looked, and there they were again in their I-can't-get enough-of-you-and-you-can't-get-enough-of-me pose, Mandy sitting on the edge of her bed, legs dangling, their arms *swaddling* each other.

"Have you ever seen anything like that, Mother?"

"Who said angel children can't have dark-brown hair, Peggie?"

"Yeah, and angel mothers can have light-brown hair too. Ya know how on Friday nights this beautician, Dave, comes over from this classy salon and cuts hair free? Well, last Friday we were all down in the pool room where he does it, and we talked Mrs. Canfield into getting her hair cut. She didn't think she wanted to, but we made her do it, and Dave cut it short and styled it so she can wash it now and not have to curl it, and it's so much easier for her while she's here. Isn't that neat?

"Mandy looks a lot younger than thirteen, don't you think? I know you always told me I'd get to an age where I'd be glad to look younger than I was, but I haven't yet, though I don't think I look as much younger as most C.F.ers do."

Peg's normal chatter—if anything could normalize me, Peg's chatter could.

And, of course, no way would I tell her that she did look as much younger as most C.F.ers did, could pass more readily for sixteen than twenty-three, or that her voice sounded younger. Or that her inner world was *younger* than the world in which she lived.

"Sometimes at night when I can't sleep, Mother, I look across the room and Mandy's sleeping and Mrs. Canfield is standing beside her bed looking down on her. I mean, as long as I'm awake, she's just standing there in the night looking down on Mandy. It would break your heart. . . . Would you take this hot chocolate down to the kitchen and heat it in the microwave, please?"

I often asked myself where Peg got her sensitivity to the feelings of others. Well, from the hurt feelings of her own childhood, I was sure, and from the hurt feelings of the most hurtful period of her life—junior high. How she had endured junior high I did not know, with the boys who waylaid her in the hall every day chanting, "Peggie Woodson, are you dead yet?" And with the girls who sniggered when she coughed, "Cover your swamp, Woodson. You're polluting us."

Sometimes I thought I would not survive Peg's years in junior high, praying every morning that things would be better for her, but being greeted every afternoon with a new tale of woe. "These girls were following me home today, Mother, and they were shouting, 'Where does your mother buy your clothes, Peggie, at Winnie the Pooh?' Oh, Mother . . ."

Oh, Peggie . . .

Still, no matter how we tried to dress her *like everybody else*, or how long she let her hair grow, or how we curled it every morning *in the latest style*, her build was so small and childlike, she looked like she came out of Winnie the Pooh.

Yet Peg had survived junior high, not hardened, but softened, and not only to her own feelings but to the feelings of others.

◇   ◇   ◇

They closed the junior high you went to, Peg. A hospital uses the building now for community education. Your father keeps going in to see if the plaque that says you graduated with a four-point average is still on the wall. The school system keeps telling him they'll give him the plaque when they take it down, but I don't think your father wants the plaque. He just wants to make sure it's still on the wall of what was once your junior high . . .

50

Remember the time in high school, Peg, when you were identifying so with the moods of your friends, you had to find a word to describe what you were doing?

"No, Mother, not sympathizing,*" you said. "No, Mother, not* empathizing. *Those words mostly describe feeling sad, and I want a word that describes feeling happy with my friends too."*

I checked out my thesaurus. "How about fellow-feeling, *Peg?"*

"It makes me sound like a bug," you laughed, "or a pervert," but it was the best we could do.

If I'd had my wits about me, Peggie, I'd have suggested loving.

◇　◇　◇

When Peg wasn't talking that first day, or eating, or having aerosols or therapy or I.V.'s, she spent her time waiting: for Dr. Rathburn to make rounds, for John to visit, for Angie to come on duty, for friends to phone.

When Dr. Rathburn appeared in the door, she asked, "Will you excuse us, please, Mother?"

I sat on my cot—and eavesdropped. I lost track of how many times I sat on my cot and eavesdropped. I knew I was violating Peg's status as a grown child, but I had to know what was going on medically, and it was easier than tracking Dr. Rathburn down, and what can I say?

"No pessimistic comments today," Peg pronounced as the doctor, self-proclaimed pessimist of the hospital staff, walked in the room.

"Okay," Dr. Rathburn nodded, turned heel, and walked out of the room, Peg's giggle tagging after him.

So much for covert surveillance that first day.

John didn't stay long when he came either.

"He's finishing his senior year at Cleveland State, Mother, full course load, and he got this great chance to take a full-time job, so he took it, school being almost over, and he has to practice every week with the Cleveland Orchestra Chorus."

I walked John out when he left, all six feet of him, with

his brown-haired, freckle-faced, boyish, wholesome, Irish look. He didn't much care for the wholesome part. "Someday I'm going out and do something decadent," he'd laugh.

But he wasn't laughing that first day as we walked to the elevator, his young face bared to fear as only an uninitiated young man's face can be. "She's going to be all right, Mrs. Woodson," he said. "I know deep down that everything is going to be all right."

It's hard to be young. I wished that I could help John, but it's hard to help the young.

Joe and I had been young once, back before anything really bad had happened to us, back in the arrogance of our youth when we were sure that nothing really bad ever would. Back during my second pregnancy when people told us they had *this feeling* that this child would be healthy, and we had the feeling too. And nine years back when people told us they had *this feeling* that Joey would not die; some even said: "God told us that Joey is not going to die." And twenty-three years back—before I could spell cystic fibrosis.

I didn't want to be young again, but I didn't like being old either.

◇   ◇   ◇

Joanne Avellone checked in then and was all Peg had said she would be, a compact kind of girl with shortish dark hair curling under at the ends, an asthmatic eighth grader with prednisone chipmunk cheeks and a dear grin. She wore red sweats most of the time, and, no, she said, the room wasn't too cold for her.

From the beginning she jumped to answer the phone before Peg or I could get to it. "I'll be your social secretary, Mrs. Woodson."

As with Mandy, I loved Joanne from the start.

She reminded me of Peg at her age, so straight she didn't fit the junior high scene. She had asthma all right, so bad she dropped unconscious at times, but the doctors had some thought that she enjoyed coming into the hospital, that it was a refuge for her, as it had always been for Peg, a place where kids with physical oddities were not odd, where kids with defective bodies worked at perfecting their souls in a way that was odd outside the hospital.

The fourth floor was full of C.F. patients, all dying, most knowing what stage of dying they were in. "If you don't laugh, you're gonna cry, so you might as well laugh," they said.

"God gives you strength to handle whatever comes, Mrs. Woodson," Angie said as she swished about the room in white skirt and pale-pink blouse, sleek brown hair tossing around enormous, gorgeous brown eyes. I'd never taken to brown eyes till I met Angie's nursing-brown eyes.

"Now, see, see, isn't she neat?" Peg pressed when Angie swished out of the room. "I asked her if she had requested to be assigned to this room, but she said no, it just *happened*. You really should appreciate this room more, Mother.

"You remember, Mother, when I rented my apartment, how you told me you prayed that it would be full of light, a place of love and happiness for everyone who came there? And I agreed? Well, when you came, did you feel the peace and love of God there?"

"Yes, I did, honey. It's been a *lighted* place for me every time I've come."

"Good. Some of my friends have told me that too. Remember when we found the bright-yellow bedspread that was an exact match to my bright-yellow drapes and my bright-yellow bedroom walls? Well, you called the color scheme monochromatic, but to me it's always been a blaze of sunshine . . . I love my apartment. . . ."

And that's when I knew that Peggie was waiting for more than Dr. Rathburn and John and Angie, knew that for her this whole period of her hospitalization was a period of waiting to see if she'd go back to her apartment.

I hid my *knowing* that she would not, especially when she coughed. "I want you right here beside me, Mother, when I cough."

Oh, it was terrible, and her exhaustion afterward total. I tried to find a way to bear the *knowing* that she would not get better, not go back to her apartment. There was no way.

Midafternoon Peggie decided to go for a ride in her wheelchair, instructing me on how to work the oxygen tank on the back.

It undid me, though I tried to cover it. What if I figured wrong and the oxygen ran out? What if it stopped working? What if all of a sudden she couldn't breathe and we weren't where I could get help?

Peggie's only concern was my inability to push the wheelchair in a straight line.

How had she taken such a giant step into invalidism without my knowing it? How had she settled so effortlessly into a mode of transportation she had heretofore refused to touch with her little finger?

And as though reading my thoughts as we set off on our first wheelchair excursion, Peg said, "When you don't absolutely have to do a thing, you can't. When you do absolutely have to do a thing, you can. Watch out ahead! Out-of-control wheelchair coming through!"

We careened down to the second floor to see one of Peg's friends who was in down there. Until recently all the older C.F. patients had stayed on the fourth floor, but that was before *cepatia*. The family of bacteria that grew in C.F. lungs was called *pseudomonas*, and cepatia was a new, deadly member of that family, resistant to antibiotics and so decimating the C.F. population that while the doctors weren't sure C.F. patients could give it to each other, they weren't sure they couldn't, so they assigned patients with cepatia to the fourth floor and patients without cepatia to the second floor.

Mrs. Canfield had lost a baby to C.F., and also had a son, Bill, about Peg's age, who had C.F. Recently when Mandy and Bill were in the hospital at the same time, Mandy on four and Bill on two, they met in the stairwell between floors to visit.

"Should you be going down to two if you have cepatia, Peg?"

"Oh, I don't have cepatia."

"Well, why on earth did they put you on four?"

"I made them. I have more friends up there."

I wheeled Peg into Dave's room, an old C.F. friend, old in the length of time Peg had known him and very old in the length of time he had lived—thirty-two years.

And then I stalked down Dr. Rathburn. "What," I demanded, "is Peggie doing on four if she doesn't have cepatia?"

"Cepatia did show up on one of Peggie's X-rays during a former hospitalization, Mrs. Woodson. I'm not sure whether or not she has it now, but if I lose her, it won't be because of cepatia. She's been operating for a long time on a very small portion of good lung. When that portion goes, nothing will save her."

Which meant, *It doesn't matter whether or not Peggie has cepatia.*

I had moved from undone to unstrung by the time I got Peg back to her room, and then Joe arrived, wandering about in that aimless way he has when he has an aim in mind but doesn't want to push.

Finally he could not contain himself. "I brought my communion kit, Peg. I thought we could have communion together."

"No thank you, Father."

"What?" Joe blurted, and then assuming that Peg could not have understood, "I just had in mind the three of us having communion together. I thought you'd like that, Peggie."

"I'd rather not, Father."

Joe reeled from the room, and I followed, leading him down to the cafeteria.

"Why?" he agonized as we sat over coffee. "Why does she reject me?"

I couldn't deny that she held him off. As for why, I'd explained the why to Joe, and explained it again, and it had done no good. Joe loved his daughter as he had never loved another human being. Peggie felt possessed by that love, and Peggie would not be possessed.

"Remember how she took her first steps to me, Meg, in the driveway of the old parsonage in Tennessee? I've never forgotten that she took her first steps to me. And when the children were older and we took them to the park, she'd yell, 'Swing me higher, Father. My turn. My turn. Higher, Father.' And every Friday night when I had my night with the children, she'd report to me on how many books she read that week.

"Even the day before she started junior high, she asked me to make a trial walk with her. That was the beginning of the end, though. I know you say I shouldn't have insisted that she keep on spending Friday nights with me, but they were so special. Why was it so much to ask?"

"Ask? No, Joe, insist. Even since Peg's been in her no-touch stage, you've sneaked kisses. Oh, Joe, if you'd just let her come to you of her own accord, even now she'd come."

"I always tried to be a good father, Meg." Joe dropped his head into his hands, his voice muffled, as though he could not speak his grief in full voice to human face. "Remember the year we went to the Space Center in Florida and Peg found license plates for every state? Not every father would spend fifty-five minutes driving up and down a parking lot so his daughter could collect license plate colors."

"You've always been a good father, Joe, and Peg has always loved you. You should hear how angry she gets if anyone in the church criticizes you, and how she worries about you when you're sick, but she's not a little girl anymore. She feels controlled by the tension she produces in you if she says no to you in anything."

But Joe was hurting too much to hear anything I said. "I've been in the ministry thirty years, Meg, and the only parishioner who has refused communion is my own daughter."

I didn't know what to do except put my arm through his and press him close as we walked to the door of the hospital.

"When Peggie was a little girl, Meg, whenever I went away overnight, she smuggled a smile-face heart inside my suitcase, and it always said, *Hurry back, Father.* Whatever happened to that little girl?"

I went back to the cafeteria, sat down way in the back

facing the wall, and tried to pull myself together.

◊   ◊   ◊

When Joey died, Peg, I told myself that when a child grew up, every mother lost the child that had been. That I had not lost Joey as a baby or a little boy in a way that different, though I had lost him as a twelve-year-old boy in a way different as different could be.

I knew better when you died. Knew that the child lives on in the adult, dies with the adult. Knew that I had lost not only a twenty-three-year-old daughter, but a three-month-old daughter, a three-year-old daughter, an almost-thirteen-year-old, bright-eyed, sidling-up, coloring-book daughter.

I spent hours every day for a month after your death putting yours and Joey's pictures in albums, your father peering over my shoulder, beside myself if I couldn't tell if the picture of you in the purple quilted robe Santa left one year was taken on your tenth or eleventh Christmas. As though we could keep you alive in picture books.

You have three books, Peggie. Joey, one. No matter. Your father and I have lost all the years of you both.

Your father knows all the way through now that he doesn't have a little girl anymore. If that makes you happy, Peggie.

◊   ◊   ◊

I rode the elevator up to the fourth floor, part of me praying that Joe would get home safely but most of me roiling in rage at Peg. Oh, I knew why she held her father off, but he loved her so much—and this was not the time.

But when I got to her room, there she sat smacking away at her baked chicken. "Sometimes, Mother, when they have something I really like on the menu, I order double—*smack smack*—and save it for when they don't have anything I like. So will you ask Cherie at the desk for a sticker and take this extra plate of chicken and mashed potatoes and put it in the refrigerator with my name on it, please?"

"You can be such a snit to your father, you know that, Peggie?"

She said nothing till she had picked every particle of chicken off her chicken leg.

"Communion has never meant anything to me, Mother. I know it should, but it doesn't, and Father knows that. He didn't want to have communion for my sake, just for himself."

"If that's true, Peggie, and I don't think it is, would it have been so much to ask for you to go along with it for his sake?" I was always caught between the two of them.

"On how many occasions have I been in the hospital, Mother? We lost track a long time ago, right? And on precisely how many of those occasions has Father wanted to have communion with me? None. Right?"

She picked up her napkin and patted and patted her mouth, a super-prissy pussy cat prolonging the show. And then she put down her napkin and pushed back her tray, and though she hardly moved her lips, the words came through the slit between them with a spewing force.

"I am not," she spewed, "ready—for the last rites—yet."

I picked up her extra dinner plate and my purse, went to the kitchen, and gulped a valium.

Joanne had rented the color TV over her bed, and she and Peg spent the evening watching it and chatting and snacking and laughing.

And there was evening, and there was morning, the first day, and I saw everything that had happened, and, behold, it was real.

At eleven-thirty that night Mrs. Canfield and I stood side by side in the darkened hallway, two middle-aged women in front of a cart of distilled water filling our daughters' humidifiers side by side.

"I don't think Amanda's going to make it this time," Mrs. Canfield said.

And my heart broke for her, but all I said was, "I don't think Peggie's going to make it this time either."

But in the end, thank God, Amanda did.

7

*T*he second morning at hair-washing time, Peg said, "You can get things ready at the sink, Mother, since it seems to mean so much to you."

She sounded like she was embarking on one of her larks. *Just letting you be a mother, Mother dear. Let's not make a big deal out of this.*

But as I glanced sideways at her, I saw a look of grimness I'd not seen on Peggie's face before. *You're making too big a deal out of not making a big deal out of this, daughter dear.* I tried to keep from looking grim, but for Peg to make major hair-washing concessions two days in a row . . .

Things were whizzing by me too fast. Peg was whizzing by me too fast.

I'd watched Joey die as he lost control of his bladder, wetting his bed, a great twelve-year-old boy embarrassed beyond measure at wetting his bed. "I'll change your sheets myself, okay, Joey? Nobody will know." And then wetting his bed and not being embarrassed. And then wetting his bed and not knowing. I was going to watch Peggie die as she lost control of her hair washing. I knew it, and I knew I could not stop it, but, oh, slow down, slow down, my dear, dear daughter.

"Okay, so here's what you do, Mother. Open the door under the sink so you can put a chair there and push it in close. Then fold one towel up three times and lay it over the

59

edge of the sink for me to lean on. Then put another towel and my shampoo and conditioner and final rinse beside the sink, and a washcloth in case I get water in my eyes. And my pick. And the water should be halfway between warm and hot."

What an organized person Peggie had always been—and was now even more so. Every morning she instructed me in the arrangement of every item on every surface around her bed. She had pulled off her usual coup, confiscating the game table for her personal use, lining it up alongside her bed.

No, she didn't snap at me if I failed to position her box of straws close enough to the edge of the game table so she could reach it but not so close she could accidentally knock it off, yet I sensed her incredulity at my inefficiency in performing the simplest tasks.

Her breakfast tray that morning included coffee for me. "Usually I order two hot chocolates for myself, Mother, but from now on I'll order one. That way I won't be gypping the hospital if I order coffee for you."

How buttressed I felt on all those hospital mornings as I took those steaming sips of Peggie's thoughtfulness to me, bungling servant though I was.

◇　　◇　　◇

One thing my counselor has helped me understand is that when a person, especially an independent type like you, loses control of the big things in her life, she compensates by maintaining meticulous control of the little things. So it was natural, Peg, for you to be persnickety about your surroundings.

Did you know I've been seeing a counselor? One of the best things that's come out of your death. I'm working not only on my grief but on the low self-esteem that has always kept me from getting close to people. As long as I had you, Peg, I got by. When I didn't have you anymore, I had to get help or go under.

A lot of good things have happened as a result of your death, though nothing that makes up for The Happening.

I got my exercise in the hospital scurrying up and down the hall, one way to the teen room, the other way to the kitchen, putting something in the microwave to get hot or in the refrigerator to keep cold, or fetching drinking cups or mucus cups or towels or ice or hospital gowns from the kitchen or the supply room next door.

"How come," Peg asked that second morning, "every time you go out the door to go one way, you always go the wrong way first? I know, because then I see you come right back the other way."

"I think when I lived in with Joey his room must have been on the other side of the hall, so I turned the opposite way when I got things for him, and now I get mixed up. You know me and my sense of direction," I said, and we both chuckled, neither of us having any sense of direction.

If anything, Peg had less directional sense than I. We lived in Parma Heights, one of Cleveland's western suburbs. Try as I would to explain to Peg why, if we were farther west than our suburb, we had to go east to get to it, she'd say, "Go east to go west? I don't get it."

Or if I told her that some house was on the north side of the street, she'd say, "But didn't you tell me stuff like that depends on which way you're coming from? I don't get it."

"Well, Mother," she said now, "I know how you can be sure of going the right way every time you go out in the hall."

"How?"

"Always go out backward."

"Go backward to go forward? I don't get it."

And we were off and laughing in that raucous, rolling, belly-holding way I laughed only with Peggie and she with me, except I had laughed that way with my mother when I was Peggie's age. Still did at times.

Only it didn't last long that second morning because Peg's unmanageable laughing started her coughing in a violently unmanageable way, unnerved me so that when she stopped coughing, I ran to the bathroom so she'd not see me laughing and crying at the same time.

Peggie would never let herself laugh that way again. I

was sure of it, and before long my mother would not be around for me to laugh that way with either, and I'd be without past, and to whom would I give the fluted green vase my mother's mother had given my mother, and my mother me? I would never again have anyone in my life as much like me as Peggie. And who would care about *when I was young?*

When I was young, Peggie, I wanted to say, erupting from the bathroom, laughing, *when I was your age living in Queens and my friends and I came up out of the subway in Manhattan and they didn't know which way to turn, they'd ask me. I'd give it my most analytical shot. Then if I pointed right, they'd turn left—and left would be right.*

I wanted to keep the laughter alive. I couldn't, of course, and when I emerged from the depths, it was on feet so padded with sadness that Peg didn't hear, and she lay with such dark shades of her own sad sureness that she would never laugh that way again flickering on her face that I whirled back into the bathroom.

Yesterday had been my day of truth. Was today Peggie's day to have her flickers of truth? I thought it was so, though all she said when I came back out of the bathroom was, "Have you remembered yet which room was Joey's room, Mother?"

"No, Peg. I've tried all these years but I can't remember. How could I not remember something like that?"

"It's okay, Mom. I'll show you next time we go out. Don't worry about it, hear?"

All I said was "Okay, honey," but I knew that we had each acknowledged the other's sadness, and that *It's okay, Mom* and *Okay, honey* were enough. I knew too, that Peg had showed me Joey's room many times before, and that no matter how many times she showed me, I would not remember.

It would have been better if we could have talked openly about our feelings, but we couldn't—and it was okay.

I didn't know whether or not Joe would show up that day, but he arrived early in the afternoon with none of the half-steam-ahead air of yesterday. Nurses and doctors and patients steered clear as he full-steamed his way to Peggie's bed and cast anchor beside her.

"I looked up *hupomone* in Barclay's commentaries," he told her, his body taut, as though standing against an inevitable, ebbing tide.

"Hupomone, Father?"

"It's the Greek word for "endurance" in your quotation, Peg. Listen to this: 'In the Christian life we have a means. That means is steadfast endurance. The word is *hupomone* which does not mean the patience which sits down and accepts things but the patience which masters them. It is not some romantic thing which lends us wings to fly over the difficulties and the hard places . . . . *Hupomone* means not only the ability to bear things, but the ability, in bearing them, to turn them into glory.' "

"Wow, Father."

Joe's tension eased a bit as though maybe, this once, the line he threw out to tie Peg to himself would hold, and he continued to read: "It is always a comfort to feel that others have gone through what we have to go through . . . the prophets and the men of God could never have done their work and borne their witness had they not patiently endured."

Joe looked at Peg through anxious eyes, and she looked back at him through misty eyes, and Joe took courage to read once more. "There will be moments in life when we think that God has forgotten, but . . . *Hupomone* can breast the tides of doubt and sorrow and disaster and come out with faith still stronger on the other side."

Peggie couldn't talk for a spell, but then she said, "I appreciate your looking all that up and writing it out for me, Father."

Oh, Joe, you've done so well. Value this closeness, but stop now, Joe. Don't pull the rope too tight.

But Joe could not stop. He grabbed Peg's hand. She jerked it away. The rope broke.

At which moment a man with a hospital badge attached to his shirt sauntered into the room, and Peggie leaped out of bed and threw herself at him. "Jerry, where have you been? I've been in for a week and haven't seen you. I thought you'd never be assigned to me."

Joe sat there, adrift, watching his daughter hug this who-is-he-anyway man; and then, unnoticed by Peg, he got up and floundered down the hall again, me beside him again. "Why, Meg? Why him and not me?"

"She appreciated what you did for her, Joe," I said, and hugged him right there in front of the elevator, held his hand as we walked through the underground tunnels and into the parking garage.

"I just have to accept the fact that in the past few years I haven't had much of a relationship with Peggie. If I could only stop trying so hard, Meg. Why do I always try too hard?" And he cried then, like a boy, and I held him again, protectively, in the dusty, dusky depths of the parking garage.

"How are you doing, Meg?" he asked before he left. "Tomorrow I'll come over at suppertime and take you out. Would you like that?" And then he held me, and I broke down and sobbed with him.

Please, God, we all need hupomone.

◇　　◇　　◇

"That was Jody, from Bunting, ya know," Peggie said, hanging up the phone as I returned to the room. "When I get back to my apartment, she and Pam are going to have National Spitfire Day for me."

Spitfire had been Peg's nickname in college because, her friends said, she was naturally high, always taking off into the sky.

"Once Jody and Pam had a Valentine's party for me when I got back from the hospital, just the three of us, but with special plates and decorations. Sometimes I feel bad because I think my friends are more important to me than I am to them, like even here I visit people more than they visit me, but then something like this happens and I feel really good."

"Mrs. Canfield told me that when you were in the last time, Peg, and her Bill was in for so long, that fifteen C.F.

patients died while he was in—it was a record—and Bill was so sick and discouraged, and the only thing that cheered him up were your visits."

"Boy! Now I really feel good! I mean, I always wondered if I was making a pest of myself because he never said whether he wanted me to come or not."

And then, "You know what Father read about *hupomone*? Well, I knew all that stuff in my heart, but it's good to know it in my head, too."

Oh, Peggie, you're so sensitive to your own hurts and to the hurts of others, you can't be unaware of how bitterly you hurt your father.

Mrs. Canfield packed Mandy and wheelchair into her car and drove to the Severance Mall that afternoon, and Peg and I took off on our daily wheel around the hospital.

First to see Jillian, a C.F. friend up the hall too sick even for a wheelchair, and then down to the cafeteria, "Because, Mother, since you were here last, they lined a wall of the cafeteria with vending machines, one of which will vend one microwave popcorn, which one can pop on the occasion of one's choice." Peg had plans for the evening.

Another machine vended her an ice cream sandwich, and we sat at a table while she licked away at the sandwich's melting middle.

"It's too bad about Jillian being deaf, isn't it, Mother? That happens once in a while from the antibiotics C.F.ers take. She communicates well with her hands, though, and she and the guy she lives with really care about each other. Now don't be shocked, Mother. He's the tall, shaggy one you see in the hall with the raincoat flappin' around his legs.

"They're right out of the sixties, sitting on the floor of their apartment eating wheat germ and all. Sometimes I think it's good I wasn't old enough to be a part of that scene, because some things about it appeal to me, like all the people in *MASH* running with all their might to get to the wounded on the chopper pad. I wanna cry every time I see that. And all that good rebellion," she added, gleaming rebellion at me out of the corner of her eye.

"Once, Mother, a nurse sent me over to the Hearing Center, and instead of sending someone with me, she gave me my own chart to carry. Now you know me. I wasn't about to miss a chance like that. So I looked at my chart, and every day the nurse had written *up and socializing.* I thought they put strictly medical stuff on your chart. Anyway, these days I'm *down and socializing,* right?" she asked, patting her wheelchair and chuckling at her little joke— and not quite guarding the look of unguarded disbelief on her face.

Was there a right way to look at your daughter's guarded-unguarded look of disbelief?

When she got back to bed, she wrote "I missed you, roomie. Hurry back!" on a paper towel and asked me to put it on Mandy's bed.

Then she took another paper towel, paper towels being what one wrote on in the hospital, and sent me up the hall with a note to Jillian. "I need to go to Severance to buy shoes. How about going with me when we both stop feeling so crummy? You'd liven things up."

And Jillian wrote back, "Sounds good, but how would we get there?"

And Peggie wrote something for me to take back to Jillian, but folded the towel up. Well, being Peggie's mother, I wasn't about to miss my chance, and I unfolded the towel and read, "My mother, but it's okay. She's cool."

Cool, man, cool. I swaggered up the hall—I, Peggie Woodson's mother who was *cool.*

And even though Jillian didn't send a return message, I folded the towel up and took it away with me in the pocket of my robe. Then when Peggie was asleep, I took it out and wrote a heading across the top, "*Hot* chocolate and My mom's *cool,*" and secreted it away in the bottom of my red suitcase to be filed in the memory box at home along with Peg's girlhood affirmations of her mother.

John visited that night from seven-thirty to ten, and Peg fed him with bits and pieces of food she'd stashed away for herself.

The snack lady came around twice a day, and Peg always stocked a drawer in her bedside cabinet with Lorna Doones and Oreos and R.C. Colas, taking bags of *her loot* home with her when she left the hospital. Her hospitalization paid for the snacks, she insisted, and they were hers.

We laughed a lot as the weeks went by about how we filled John up, not an easy task, with a chicken wing, a cup of broccoli soup, rainbow sherbet, and package after package of Lorna Doones washed down by half-sized cans of R.C. Cola.

Peg had a lot of back pain and had requisitioned a water mattress for her bed, which she got out of that second night and put John in, fluffing the pillows around him, sitting beside him in a lawn chair, and inviting me to join them in munching popcorn and watching *Fame* in the living color she had rented for the occasion.

The night being an occasion because John was staying for so long, but also because of *Fame*. Peg's loyalty to the program was extreme, I think, because of the *togetherness* of the *Fame* kids as they danced and interacted in the entirety of their lives, because she interacted with them, found with them the oneness with a group she had craved her whole life long. And also, I think, because for one limber, lightsome hour a week her weighted body leaped and pirouetted with *her group*.

But, oh, the look of longing on her face that her body might, not just in fancy, fly.

I could see that Peg was drained physically when the program ended, and when John left I got her settled as quickly as I could for the night, considering the routine. I brought her a hospital gown, and she walked slowly to the bathroom to put it on and then slowly to the sink in the corner of the room to brush her teeth, during which time I arranged her bed tray: a mucus cup, covered, to cough mucus into at the front of the tray; a mucus cup, uncovered, to hold two Sucrets at the back of the tray; a cup of ice water, center right, and next to it a cup of ice that would become ice water as the original ice water became warm water; and positioned between the cups a straw, paper cover removed; and much else, all of which I never remembered.

"Okay, Peg," I said that second night, "I am going to get

your bed tray perfect." But then I forgot the box of tissues she used to wipe her nose, which dripped because of her oxygen cannula. How could I forget her big box of purple tissues? Nothing left me as witless as fiddling with the oxygen on Peg's wheelchair and fixing her bed tray at night.

I pined for a book to read when I settled into my cot. At home I always read in bed before I went to sleep. I pined for a touch of home.

Then Angie found me a flashlight, and since I couldn't read without a pencil in hand, I held my book in one hand, a pencil in the other, and the flashlight under my chin. Peggie and Angie and Joanne laughed at me a lot about that as the nights passed.

The book was the one I'd thrown into my suitcase at 7:20 in the morning that nonhospital world ago. I had bought the book some time before at the Jesuit Retreat House I go to for silence and solitude, had felt nudged to buy it.

Usually when I was at the Retreat House, I took all the books I might want to buy to my room and browsed through them before deciding, but this book I bought without opening its covers. *Abandonment to Divine Providence* by Jean-Pierre de Daussade, a seventeenth-century priest-professor.

A deep book, I discovered now, as I leafed through it, getting the hang of holding on to the flashlight with my chin—a book written in small sections, each section headed by a single sentence. Mostly I read the headings—one of them over and over—and later when Peggie called for me in the night, I read it to her:

> The more God takes from the abandoned soul, the more is he really giving it . . . the more he strips us of natural things, the more he showers us with supernatural gifts.

"Wow, Mother. Can you believe that? Like . . . could this be a sign . . . that I really am . . . like living out the quotation? What with Father reading about it today and all? Come on, come on, whaddaya think? Where did you get that book? What kind of book is it?"

The look of wonder on Peg's face dispelled all the other looks I'd seen on her face that day: the grimness and the sadness, the disbelief and the longing to fly.

"I think God has given us a handbook, Peg," I said. "I think God has given us both a handbook."

8

I remember three things about Friday, my third wake-up-in-the-hospital day: that the Lerneys visited; that Ronnie and Lonnie, twin C.F. boys from down the hall visited; and that Angie changed the dressing on Peggie's broviac.

After the first three days, the days run together in my mind, till the last three days. Strange how the details of the shock-days of our life stick in our mind, straight up, in perpetuity, however hard we try to knock them down into oblivion.

Anyway, I remember that the Lerneys arrived late in the morning of the third day of Peg's last hospitalization: Andy, an exceedingly tall, dark-haired man who had been Peg's journalism professor at college, and Lou, an enjoyably short, dark-haired woman who worked with retarded adults.

At the moment they had seven children—I think it was seven—biological, adopted, foster. Actually, it was eight if you counted Peggie, and you had to count Peggie when you counted Lerney children.

Peg picked up families the way a compulsive overeater picked up Mars bars from a vending machine in the hospital cafeteria. Like the Dominor family she picked up in New York when she spent her freshman year at John Huss College. The Dominors had three younger children, one with

C.F. Peggie was their *college kid.*

Then there was her Washington family. Several sum-mers ago Peg had moved into the hospital for six weeks to take care of Marilyn, a C.F. friend whose family lived in Washington state and could only be with her on an on-off basis. Twice now, once before and once after Marilyn's death, Peg had flown to the West Coast to be with her Wash-ington family.

And then at Bunting College she joined the Lerney fam-ily, sleeping over one night a week at their home, vacation-ing with them. She'd refused to vacation with Joe and me since she was sixteen, but not only did she spend a week tenting with the Lerneys—bug-hating Peggie *tenting* with the Lerneys—but two weeks trailering with the Dominors.

"What time will you be home for Easter, Peg?" I had asked last year.

"Oh, I'm spending Easter with the Dominors, Mother. It's only a nine-hour drive. I don't consider Easter a family holiday."

But she did. She considered it a holiday to be spent with her New York family.

Did Peg know how abandoned Joe and I felt when she drove off to the Dominors for Easter?

"What's this strange raincoat doing in the hall closet?" I asked after the Easter incident.

"Oh, that belongs to Dominor Grandmother," Peg an-swered smugly. "Dominor Grandmother was afraid I'd get cold coming home and made me put it in the car. What did you guys do for Easter anyway? Go out to a restaurant to eat? Why should I come home for that?"

Well, to ease our loneliness, Peg? To bring us a pot of purple tulips? To wear your pretty blue dress and go out to a restau-rant with us so we could be a family?

Oh, Peg knew how we felt when she took off to New York for Easter or to Washington for Thanksgiving—else why the cruelty of her defense?

"Why everybody else's family and not ours?" Joe ago-nized, and I told myself Peg could go to New York and stay there for all I cared, agony and anger being related emotions—agony and anger and love.

I should have told Peg she could go to New York and stay, but what if she did? And what if, before I had a chance to take back my dismissal of her, death dismissed her forever from my life?

Still, I understood something of the reasons for Peg's actions. No members of our extended family lived nearby, and not many friends came and went in our home. Peggie gravitated toward families with lots of kids and grandmas and uncles and cousins. She needed to belong, and you didn't belong anywhere like you belonged in an extended family.

Especially if you had a bad case of what Peg and I laughingly called her *peer panic*. She never had gotten over the isolation we imposed on her in her preschool days, lest she catch something from the other children; when, indeed, the lasting case of alienation she caught had damaged her more than any cold could have. She never had gotten over the sense of differentness she imposed on herself in elementary school because of her *terrible cough* and her *skinny arms*. Nor had she ever recovered from the mockery of the kids in junior high.

Yes, she'd had good friends starting in ninth grade Advanced English and through high school and college. Yet there were never enough friendships and they were never deep enough. Many times I'd watched a relaxed Peggie smiling, chatting—till one of her peers walked by. So many times I'd stiffened with her as she patted her hair, smoothed her pants—and looked the other way. I folded on the inside whenever I stiffened with Peg on the outside.

Always anxious for me to meet her families, she was ecstatic that the Lerneys had come to the hospital while I was there.

"And here at long last we have Andy and Lou Lerney, Mother," she announced, wearing her Tae Kwon Do T-shirt and making chopping motions with her hands as she drew us together. "The Lerneys understand how stuff bothers my lungs, so when they know I'm coming, they vacuum the house and dust and put out the cats. Is that neat or what?"

"That's neat in more ways than one," I said, and could see Peg was at least not humiliated by my unsophisticated wit.

The Lerneys sat on one side of Peg's bed and I on the other, and while the conversation flowed around me, I felt a part, not only of this small group but of the larger family group of which they talked.

"How's Greg?" Peg asked, explaining to me that Greg was the nine-year-old who always waited for her at the front door and yelled and screamed and grabbed hold of her when she got there and tipped up the chair next to his at the table to reserve it for her.

"And what about Katie? Oh, no, she ran away again? You had to call the police again? How embarrassing. And Lisa already has a date for the senior prom? Who with? Who with?" And then, looking obliquely at her former journalism prof, "I mean to say, of course, With whom? With whom?"

I walked Lou and Andy to the elevator when they left.

"We thought this was a routine hospitalization," they said, "but, oh, how weak she is, and that cough. We had no idea things could get so bad so fast." How *they* loved *her.*

"Things don't look good," I said, was desperate to say to someone who cared about Peg as only family cared. "I'll keep you posted," I promised, and felt so cleansed from the aloneness of my worry that I walked back down the hall scrubbing the tears from my cheeks like a rarely included child myself, unexpectedly chosen.

"Why did you walk them to the elevator?" Peg demanded. "What did you tell them?"

"Walking your visitors to the elevator is like seeing company to the door at home, Peg."

"Did you hear them say I was the only one of *their* kids doin' well right now? Me, here in the hospital, the only one of *their kids* they're not having problems with? Aren't they neat? Aren't you impressed that they drove an hour and a quarter to see me? Aren't you glad you met them?"

"Yes, Peg, I am glad." And after that morning I was at least more glad than I had been for all Peg's families.

No, Joe and I were not enough for her, and neither were her friends. In a normal life, Peg would be moving on to establish her career or her own husband-and-children family, as were most of her friends, who were vowing to husband or wife loyalty higher than their loyalty to her, moving away from her geographically and emotionally.

Peggie had a knack for knowing what she had to do to survive the detachment she felt from healthy humanity, and if struggling to keep on top of her loneliness blunted her sensitivity to bruises inflicted on mother and father, well, struggling to keep your head above water when life was sucking you under could do that.

◇   ◇   ◇

Coming to understand—not condone but understand— Peg's sometime *pushing under* of Joe and me helped me understand her pushing away, for different reasons, of Ronnie and Lonnie when they shuffled in early in the afternoon from two rooms down the hall.

"Whadda we do, Peggie," they mumbled, two slouching fourteen-year-olds with identical red cowlicks looking to an older woman for advice, "if we take chickies to the movies and everybody's smokin'? How do we get the tickets without coughin'?"

"You send your *chickies* in to get the tickets," Peg tsked, "and then you make a beeline through the lobby into the theater."

"But then we'd hafta tell them somethin's wrong with us," the would-be Romeos whined, "and they wouldn't wanna go out with us again."

Peggie didn't say anything, but she looked her disdain, and Ron stepped on Lon's heels in an effort to get out of the room fast, and Lon punched Ron two rooms down the hall to safety.

"They're jerks," Peg scoffed. "Wimps and jerks. I can't stand them."

Peg either welcomed people or wrote them off, the writing-off part her major fault. She didn't do it often, but when she did, she wrote with a heavy hand.

75

"I mean, I cannot stand people who go around feeling sorry for themselves, and I cannot stand stupid people. How can they spend their lives getting upset about stuff like buying movie tickets?"

◇   ◇   ◇

Often in the past the nurses had put Peggie in a room with someone they thought she'd be good for. "Dawn's depressed, Peg. We thought you'd be the one to cheer her up."

"Boy, Mother, isn't that something, their thinking I might help? Like giving me a mission."

"Cindy's so shy, Peggie, she won't leave her room. Would you see what you can do to get her out of there?"

Peg had Cindy out in the hall at midnight pressing her face flat against the windows of rooms that still had lights on. "You know how weird that looks from the inside, Mother? The kids practically flew out of their beds. Cindy's a slow learner, but she sure learned to do that fast. She's in high school, but her mother says I'm her first friend. I'm glad I can be her friend.

"Sometimes when I'm here," she boasted, "I feel less like a patient than a member of the staff."

Peg had her own brand of labels for the characteristics she could not accept in people. *Jerks* were people who wouldn't *try* to use the intelligence they had, wouldn't *strive* for efficiency. Peggie didn't care if someone didn't have friends; and as much as she liked faces to smile, she didn't care if someone was depressed. *Wimps* were people who wouldn't *try* to overcome their friendlessness or their depression. Peggie could not stand people who did not have spunk.

"It's not that I don't like Ronnie and Lonnie. It's just difficult to be around them," she said that third afternoon, and that was the closest she came to understanding her aversions.

I hoped to the end that she would learn to be more tolerant. She didn't.

Perhaps she couldn't. Given the extreme dependence her disease had imposed on her, perhaps she could not wrench

76

herself free of Joe and me without cruelty. And perhaps she could not resist the almost irresistible temptation to feel sorry for herself and give up on her C.F. except by the spurning of all who sniveled and couldn't manage the complications cystic fibrosis brought into their lives.

◇　　◇　　◇

Remember how you used to phone, Peggie, and ask me to spend a couple days with you in your apartment? How close we felt as we created your native *habitat together, or nested* together in the cozy, cluttered, basement habitat we created. You called me surprisingly often to come to Bunting. It comforts me when I think of the occasions you preferred to be with your other families, to remember the occasions when you wanted to be with me. For months after you died, when the phone rang, just for a minute I'd think, Maybe it's Peggie wanting me to come to Bunting . . . and then I died a bit.*

The thing is, Peg . . . the reason I worry about all this so much . . . is that I'm still not sure about how much you loved me, and now I wonder how I ever will be sure.

◇　　◇　　◇

Peggie had always been such a natural-born fighter. I, who knew her as well as anyone, had failed to appreciate till that third day in the hospital how hard she fought to stay that way—through her acceptances and her rejections—how hard she fought to fight. And even then I didn't fully appreciate it till late in the afternoon when Angie changed her broviac dressing.

◇　　◇　　◇

Oh, Peg, I wish you hadn't had such a hard way to go. I almost wish I didn't know how hard a way you had to go.

◇　　◇　　◇

Peg had run out of veins for simple I.V. hookups several hospitalizations ago, her veins so worn by antibiotics that they collapsed as soon as Dr. Rathburn inserted a needle in them. And so she had moved from simple I.V. hookups to central lines, tubing that ran through veins, generally in her upper arms, to the large vein outside her heart. Once she had a central line sticking out of her jugular vein.

"I bet you think it's gross, don't you, Mother?"

"Oh, no, honey, I don't think it's gross." And the way they bandaged it, it wasn't.

But then during her hospitalization before this one she had run out of veins that would hold even a central line, and a surgeon had implanted a broviac permanently in her chest—a length of tubing that didn't run through a vein but from an opening in her chest directly to the vein outside her heart.

No one told her that she'd have to change the dressing on her broviac every day or that the process involved different-sized gauze bandages and different sizes of tape and tubes of ointments and bottles of solutions and sterile scissors and syringes and heparin with which to flush out the broviac.

She couldn't go anywhere overnight without taking all this paraphernalia with her. She couldn't go anywhere anytime without a pair of clamps on her person lest the cap come off the tubing and she bleed to death.

"You probably should know, Mother, that if the opening gets infected and the infection whooshes to your heart, you're dead from that too. Also, if a blood clot forms at the opening and whooshes to your heart, you're dead from that."

They'd told her about the whooshing-to-your-heart part, and she had not made the decision to have the surgery lightly, obtaining duplicates of the material that would be used, laying the tubing out on a dark T-shirt in the route it would follow in her chest. Then she'd taken pictures of the T-shirt and passed them around to friends who came to the hospital to visit.

"Now, see, about five inches of the tubing, or catheter, as those of us initiated to hospital talk put it, will be on the outside, and this is the cap."

And then she named her broviac, submerging herself in

a book of names Dr. Rathburn brought in to her, her thesis being that people, and broviacs, tended to live up to their names, to the official meaning of their names, and to the personalities people expected other people, and broviacs, with certain names to have.

And so, after consultations with doctors and nurses and friends, she christened her broviac *Alexis*, "helper of mankind."

Angie was the only nurse Peg let change Alexis' dressing, and that third afternoon she asked me to watch in case I had to do it when Angie wasn't around.

I'd seen the broviac once before, when Peg had changed the dressing in her apartment. "I bet you think it's gross, don't you, Mother?"

"Oh, no, honey, I don't think it's gross." But, oh, how gross that *plastic pipe* looked protruding from the soft girlish skin between the swell of her slight boyish breasts.

Goodness knows, C.F. had done worse to her body. From the day she was born, C.F. had been killing her body, but given C.F., even the killing was a physical thing done to a physical thing. But this unnatural *thing* Peg had named—but I could not name—violated my daughter's body, and it violated my spirit. And I knew from the way she projected her revulsion onto me that it violated her spirit too. And, as always, her pain hurt me worst of all.

I hadn't been able to clear my mind of the scene in her apartment. Peggie, naked from the waist up, standing at the kitchen counter, all the boxes and bottles spread out in front of her, that *thing* pouring out of her. Nor had I been able to clear my mind of the knowledge that she stood so every day taking gentle care of the violence done her.

◇　◇　◇

I lied to you, Peggie. The only time in your life I remember lying to you. I want to tell you that I lied, to make it right. Your broviac was gross. Your broviac was abhorrent to me, Peggie.

◇　◇　◇

And it was still abhorrent to me in the hospital as Angie explained how you rolled the betadine swabs away from the opening, and what you sterilized with hydrogen peroxide, and the order of the medicines and coverings that went on under the final elastoplase. If Peg felt better thinking that in an emergency I could change the dressing, fine— but I could not.

When all was done, Alexis said, "Thank you, Angie," in a baby voice. And I thought, Aha, the pictures, the name, the voice were Peg's way of humanizing this inhuman appendage to her body—her own Peggie way of befriending her broviac.

"I notice you have your broviac case under your bed, Peggie."

"Yeah. I use hospital supplies while I'm here, but my case is here too."

After Peg had had her broviac surgery, we'd gone shopping together for a cosmetic case she could stock with her broviac supplies, and we found just what she wanted in a discount store, an azure-blue Samsonite case. But even in the discount store, it cost $80.00, an $80.00 neither she nor I could afford.

So we checked out K-Mart to see if they had something similar in a cheaper make, but they had nothing similar. Then we tried Penney's, but they had no cosmetic cases in their luggage department that day.

By this time Peg was bent with fatigue and we were turning for home when the saleswoman said, "They might still have a couple cosmetic cases on the clearance table in hardware, but the mirrors in the tops are broken."

And there they glowed, two azure-blue Samsonite cosmetic cases, duplicates of the $80.00 ones—at $15.00 apiece.

"But you don't need a mirror, Peggie. We can easily take the broken glass out." I almost bawled.

Peggie did bawl—in the middle of Penney's hardware department, second floor, Parmatown Mall.

And, as though once again Peg had been following my thoughts, she said, "Why do you suppose He put two of them on the clearance table?"

"I don't know, Peggie. Maybe to make doubly sure you knew how much He wanted you to have your special case."

"Yeah. That's probably it."

◇   ◇   ◇

Mrs. Canfield told me that as cystic fibrosis progressed in Mandy, Mandy looked aghast at her body and said, "Lookit what it's doin' to me now."

They all did that. But they moved on.

When Dr. Rathburn made rounds after the dressing changing, I heard, from my cot, Peg telling him how glad she was she'd had the broviac surgery last time she was in when she wasn't feeling as crummy as she was now, and how great it was not to be stuck with needles anymore.

Peggie handled what C.F. did to her by thinking ever-positively. Peggie handled what C.F. did to her by human-izing, and by *divinizing* what it did.

"Have you found any more good stuff in your book, Mother?" she asked that third afternoon, and I read: "God reveals himself to us through the most commonplace happenings in a way just as mysterious and just as truly and as worthy of adoration as in the great occurrences of history and the Scriptures."

And when I dared look at Peg's face, her eyes were so wide and luminous it seemed that her whole face glowed with an azure-blue light.

Oh, Peggie, shine—learn to be kind—but, oh, my coping *Peggie Woodson, shine.*

9

Oh, I do remember something else about the third day in the hospital, the third night really. How could I not remember that Joe came over as he had promised and took me out to dinner? He thought only of what he could do for me that night, and I was so used to taking care of someone else, I couldn't believe how good it felt to have someone else taking care of me.

Joe stuck his head in Peg's room. "I'm here to take your mother out, Peggie." *Lest you think I'm here to see you, Peggie. Before you can turn me away again, Peggie.*

Oh, he would risk being turned away again. Joe had a relentless capacity to open himself up to Peg's woundings—but not here, not again so soon.

To me it seemed an act of heroism for Joe to stand straight in the hall and wave gaily to Peg as though he had no wounds, so that the knowledge that she had wounded him would not wound her. I didn't know whether Joe's restraint was better for either him or Peggie than confrontation would have been, only that it was born of his fierce father-love for her, and that it wounded me to watch it, and that I loved him fiercely for it.

My friend Jan had gone through our house and packed a second suitcase for me, my list in hand, and I dressed up as best I could, feeling almost shy with Joe as we drove away from the hospital and he folded his hand over mine on the car seat between us.

We drove a mile or so to Little Italy, the only place near the hospital-university area where we could go safely at night. Little Italy, home of the Mafia, was the most crime-free neighborhood in Cleveland, the Mafia not deeming it sporting to perpetrate its dastardly deeds in its own neighborhood, and no one else deeming it *strategic* to do so.

So while the streets surrounding the hospital were empty of people at night, we found ourselves pushing our way through mobs of people laughing and arguing and jostling each other up and down the almost vertical incline that was Little Italy.

"There's a pizza parlor, Joe. Will that do?"

"No," said Joe. "You know how you feel better about yourself when you eat someplace with cloth tablecloths and candles." And grandly he led me to the Roman Villa.

He would lead me to every *fancy* restaurant in Little Italy before Peg's hospitalization was over. "What's linguine? . . . What's linguine alle vongole bianche?" we asked, till we convinced ourselves we were ordering like natives.

And when our stress was such that we needed friends to laugh with, "Saluto, amicos," Joe called to people sitting nearby, and though he called softly in deference to hushed atmospheres, the amicos and amicas for tables around laughed with us when Joe did that.

I didn't feel guilty about leaving Peg, as I did leave her emotionally as well as physically when we left for Little Italy, because I was so much better a caretaker when I returned to her. Later, of course, I didn't leave her in any way.

After dinner on our first visit to Little Italy, we ambled down the hill arm in arm "getting each other back," as Joe put it, when I noticed a few people entering a massive, moldering church across the street.

"It must be time for mass, Joe," I said, and needed to say no more. Joe knew how much it meant to me to worship in a church where I could kneel, how God *came to me* in the solemnity and majesty of the Catholic service.

"I'll wait for you outside," he said, not able himself to

worship in a church called Holy Rosary.

But, oh, how *mystical* it was inside. I was aglow with the Presence when I returned to Peg.

"What happened to the lines on your face, Mother?"

"Well, your father took me to an elegant restaurant and then I went to mass."

"Good. I'm glad you could do those things."

"Food for the body and food for—"

"You don't have to spell it out for me, Mother." Peg munched away on the breadsticks I'd brought back with me.

"—and food for the soul and both in appropriate settings," I finished rapid-fire.

◇   ◇   ◇

Every time I knelt in Holy Rosary during your hospitalization, Peg, God opened His arms and took me in—into love and truth and beauty, into the heart of things. Into His heart.

You'd like Ben, my counselor, Peggie. One thing Ben's helped me see is that I need to be more involved in intellectual and cultural activities, to feed my hunger for truth and beauty. My inclination is to work, work. I could get by with work, work while I had you, but not since I haven't had you. You should see me scooting off to the Cleveland Ballet and the Cleveland Art Museum and to Severance Hall to hear the Cleveland Orchestra.

Severance Hall is too close to the hospital for comfort, though I'm glad I've at least driven past the street you turn down to get to the hospital now. And I've started taking workshops in human behavior.

I get so excited after a workshop, and I remember how learning thrilled you and how you cried with me each Christmas when we watched The Nutcracker *ballet. I miss not sharing these things with you so much that sometimes I want to stop doing them, but then I read the quotation for the month on my C. S. Lewis calendar: "All joy reminds. It is never a possession, always a desire for something longer ago or further away or still 'about to be.' "*

And I remind myself that just as the art and music and understanding of psychology that fill such needs in me now are shadows of the fulfillment I experience when God fills me, so the presence of God I know now is a pale shadow of the about-to-be beauty and truth and love that is for you as you see God face-to-face.

But I have a way to go yet in holiness, Peggie, because my basic feeling is not gladness for you but sadness for me.

◇　◇　◇

"This kid from down the hall came to visit me while you were out, Mother," Peg said, looking at me in that way she had when she was going to talk me into doing something I was going to resist doing. "He had cancer a while ago, and they amputated his left arm. One reason I like him so much is that the first time I saw him, he said, all nonchalant-like, 'Did you know me when I had two arms?' Isn't that neat?" *Munch-munch.*

"His mother is very nice and very religious, but she won't let him listen to Christian rock, so here's what you do. Take these tapes of mine down to 410, peek in the door, and if his mother's not there, sneak them in to him."

"How old is he?"

"Thirteen."

"Well, I don't know, Peg, if his parents don't approve—"

"Come on, Mother. God comes to people in different ways, like to you at mass—and you a minister's wife! Do you have any idea how weird that seems to some people? Well, God comes to me through my Christian rock, and God comes to this kid through Christian rock when he can get his hands on it." *Munch.*

I smuggled the contraband back and forth between Peg and *the kid* five times that night, a shy, eager, gentleman-kid. I liked coming to know him as the night progressed, and I liked feeling close to Peggie the way we always felt close when we broke bread or rules together. Or *talked deep* together.

"Ya know how I've had a series of best C.F. friends through the years, Mother, and they've all died? Well, sometimes I've hoped a little that one of them might *appear* to me. Remember how we promised each other that whoever died first would come back, if she could, and tell the other what heaven was like? Well, that's what I hoped for with my friends, but none of them has come back. I have this feeling that it would be too hard for them. . . . Do you understand what I mean?"

"I suspect, Peggie, that once someone enters into heaven's perfect love, coming back to earth's puny love would make them mad."

"Boy, is it neat to have a mother who understands what I mean even when I don't understand what I mean."

◇　◇　◇

Is that why you haven't come back, Peg? I've waited, knowing that you could finagle it if anyone could. Sometimes when I'm writing this book, I think how nice it would be if you'd let me know that you're pleased.

The sober part of me says no even to that—that if you came back once, I'd wait for you to come back again. That your coming back would not help me accept your goneness. *And you are gone, Peggie.*

I'll try not to call you back, even for a momentary celebration of your book. How could I call you of all people back from enough *love?*

I will see you again, though. You may not come to me, but one day I will come to you.

◇　◇　◇

"You know all the tornadoes that have been hitting Ohio this week, Peg? Well, when we were in the restaurant, I asked your father when a tornado touched down, if he thought God said, 'Hit that house. Miss that car. Hit . . . miss.' And your father said, 'When a tornado touches down, God says, *Get in the basement.*' "

"Yeah?" Peg was getting drowsy.

"I thought it was a little funny."

"Oh, well, I guess it was a *little* funny. . . . Is Father coming tomorrow?"

"I have no idea, Peggie."

"Oh." Her voice was small.

Could it be that while Peg did not mind backing away from her father, she did mind her father backing away from her? *Dear God, let it be.*

Peg went to sleep quickly that third night, but I could not sleep. For once I wanted Peg to wake up and call me, to continue our talk-time. How would I survive the loss of this closeness? *Oh, God, the loss of my second child?* As my mind tossed and turned, it would turn nowhere but to where it was forbidden to turn—to our trip home after Joey's final hospitalization.

The nurses had packed up Joey's room while Dr. Rathburn talked to Joe and me down the hall. "There's nothing I can say when a child dies, Reverend and Mrs. Woodson." How real he was. "Do you want to spend a few minutes with Joey when the nurses are finished with him?"

"No, there's no need for that. That's not Joey. That's only Joey's body." How unreal we were.

So they took his body away without our saying a final good-bye, and Marcia, one of the two nurses who was still on the floor now, helped us down to the car with boxes jammed with the puzzles and models and Hardy Boys books and flat pajamas of a twelve-year-old boy.

The thing I remembered most about that homecoming was the pure, breaking love on Peg's fourteen-year-old face as she ran to me. "I'm sorry, Mama. Oh, Mama, I'm so sorry."

She was so stalwart, too, helping us lug the boxes into the house and dump them in my study. Incredible, the paraphernalia a twelve-year-old boy accumulated in the hospital.

"Did he really say I could have any of his books and toys I wanted? I mean, did you put the words in his mouth, or did he say it on his own? Like . . . did he really think of me just before . . . Oh, Mama."

We wrapped our arms around each other—and held on.

How would I survive the trip home from Peggie's final hospitalization without Peggie in the family room waiting for me, without her look of love, without her courage, without the consolation of her sorrow? *Oh, Peggie, how will I survive the second time around?*

And it was as though I could hear her tell me, "Well, it will be your second time around. You'll be more experienced, Mother."

As the night wore on, I realized that in her find-something-good-in-the-worst-situation way, she was right. I'd never watched anyone die before Joey—no adult, no child of mine. Part of the awfulness had been the unknownness of it. I didn't know how it would happen. . . . I knew it would not happen. . . . When would it happen? . . . God would not let it happen. . . . God betrayed me when it happened. . . . It was my fault.

I lost innocence when Joey died. It would be easier with innocence lost to watch a child die in a world where innocence was lost.

No, I never would watch a child of mine die for the first time again. I would never make a last trip home from the hospital for the first time again. Comfort? . . . Comfort.

I had made it the first time, and I would make it the second time. And maybe one day, on down the road, when I came upon someone I wasn't sure I'd come upon before, I'd say, all nonchalant-like, "Did you know me when I had two kids?"

And maybe—even if I weren't nonchalant—Peggie would hear from her golden heights and lean over the banister of heaven with a small brown-haired boy by her side and say, "Look, Joey, isn't our mother neat?"

◇   ◇   ◇

Oh, Peggie, it's too much. I'm sorry, but I'm not sure I will make it. It was easier in some ways to watch you die, but—I have no children now.

Can you hear me, Joey? Are you all right? Has someone been taking good care of you? Don't think I don't still miss you because I'm taken up with Peg right now. I try to imagine how you must look—not skinny or pale or wearing your glasses—but I don't even know if you're still a twelve-year-old boy. . . . Are you still a twelve-year-old boy, Joey?

10

$\mathcal{S}$omewhere in the two and a half weeks that were left of Peg's first three weeks in the hospital, Karol's health improved—Karol, our sickle-cell-anemia room-mate—and her mother went home nights to tend to other children. I tended to Karol.

Her arm leaned heavily on my arm as we inched our way kitty-corner across the room to the bathroom. What a feeling, the arm of another mother's child pressed into mine. How effortlessly you come to love someone you take care of physically. By the first morning, Karol was calling me *Nighttime Mama*, and another mother's child, and not even a C.F. child, was my child too.

The first morning Karol felt better, everybody in the room felt better.

And somewhere in those two and a half weeks, Peg began to put on her call light at bedtime.

"Yes, luv?" asked Cherie at the nurses' station.

"Good night, Cherie."

"Good night, luv."

What a sound. How *tucked in* the room felt when Cherie whispered, "Good night, luv."

And once at suppertime when Jan came over to eat with me in the cafeteria and I became uneasy about Peg, we gathered up our salisbury steak and butternut squash and carried it upstairs to eat with her.

But when we got to the door of room 420, what a sight! John sitting on the edge of Peg's bed facing her, his arm hooked through hers. My heart stood still at the sight of Peg and John *linked*. My heart stood still at the look on Peggie's face—bliss.

"I don't think you had to worry," Jan said as we backed down the hall, juggling our squash and coffee—and blueberry pie. "Are you sure nothing romantic is going on there?"

Everybody asked that. But while there was no romance going on there, there was love a-plenty, and when I look back on what was left of the first half of Peg's hospitalization, it's the sounds of love I hear, the sights of love I see. It's love I touch.

Peg and I both knew an *arm-to-armness* in that period that I, at least, had never known—with those *at home* behind the address 420, with the patients and parents and nurses in *the neighborhood*, and with those who visited from what seemed far-off places to give us news of their worlds and to receive news of ours.

◇　◇　◇

When I force myself, Peg, I can remember that more and more often in that period you leaned over a pillow on your bed tray to ease your breathing, as I had seen so many C.F. patients lean over a pillow in the weeks before their deaths.

And that sometime in there you said, "My hair can get by with conditioner, Mother. Forget my final rinse." I know that I'm dissociating from much that happened in the period of your hospitalization between initial shock and final trauma. I don't care. I need to feel safe again. I need the comfort of remembered love.

◇　◇　◇

Not long into the two and a half weeks, Karol moved to a room down the hall. I understood why when I visited her, for she kept the room as hot as we kept ours cold. She'd piled on the blankets in our room but never stopped shivering and never said a word. I didn't take care of her at night after she moved, but she didn't stop calling me *Night-time Mama.*

We missed Karol, but those of us left felt even closer to each other.

Mrs. Canfield rarely left Mandy, never left unmet any need Mandy had, so Peg and I didn't often have Mandy to ourselves. But one afternoon Mrs. Canfield went off for an hour or two, and I helped the little one into her wheelchair and brought her over to our side of the room.

How eagerly Joanne and Peggie and I gathered round in the space between Joanne's and Peggie's beds, Mandy enthroned in her frilly shorty gown—What else would Mandy wear?—and smiling her sweet-joyous smile.

What a comradely time we had, pressed into a tight circle, Mandy and Joanne comparing sticker collections, exaggerating their shock that Peggie and I had never heard of sticker collections.

"It helps me understand how you get out-of-date so quickly, Mother," Peg said, and everybody laughed.

Mrs. Canfield and I didn't communicate much verbally, but I was always aware of how Mandy was doing, and she was always aware of how Peggie was doing, and we were each tuned in to how the other was holding up.

"Take a break," I'd say. "Joanne and I will keep an eye on Mandy." Mrs. Canfield didn't offer to keep an eye on Peggie when I took a break. She just did, no matter how many more breaks I took than she.

"Don't worry about it, Mother," Peg said. "She doesn't have anything else to do." Which was how Mrs. Canfield made you feel.

"I hope you appreciate what a great room this is, Peggie."

One thing I tried to do for Joanne was build her self-esteem. I was good at that, having specialized in helping my children feel good about themselves.

"I love those outfits you wear, Joanne. The red contrasts beautifully with your dark hair."

Or I'd say to Peg, not looking at Joanne but speaking just loudly enough for her to hear, "Joanne's so helpful and cheerful and mannerly, I wonder if she fits in at school."

And Peg entered in, using the same words I'm sure she didn't remember I had spoken to her when she was in junior high: "Joanne's differentness makes her special, Mother, above the ordinary. But it's hard to be different, even when it's better, when you're in junior high. She just has to hang in there. She'll find kids like her to bum around with in high school."

When Joanne finally went home, I helped her mother and her sister cart her gear down to the parking lot. Saying good-bye made me cry.

I'd been a loner for so long, I was amazed when people reached out to me, or when I reached out to people. How much, I wondered, of the effort I was making with people was in response to Peg's example? Peg, who continued to call greetings to, send messages to, visit all the patients she knew on the floor, "except for the wimps, Mother." Peg, who daily told all the nurses how glad she was they were assigned to her. Peg, who greeted outside visitors as though they were of royal blood.

"Who's my nurse today, Mary? You? Oh, great!"

"Sandy, I can't believe I got you four days in a row. You can take it easy again, Mother. You know how efficient Sandy is."

Or, "Angie!" Just, "An—gie!"

"Brad, ya know Marilyn's brother from Oregon, only he's going to school in Wooster, is coming to visit this afternoon. Yah!! He's bringing his girlfriend. Yah!! I mean, I don't know her, but if she's Brad's girlfriend, I'm sure I'll like her. . . . John can only stay a few minutes tonight, Mother. Angie's fixing him supper in her apartment. Is that neat or what?"

My heart sank. "How do you really feel about that, honey?"

"Well, good. Whaddaya think? And whaddaya mean, *really*? John deserves it. . . . I have so many flowers, Mother. Why don't you take one flower from each arrangement and give one to Mandy—'The pink's to match your new shorty gown, Mandy. I like it a lot.'—and one to Jillian and one to *the kid* and one . . . oh, why not? One to Ronnie and Lonnie. No, better give them each one to keep them from killin' each other."

"Have you noticed, honey, that the nurses who used to be the closest to you don't have long talks with you anymore? They can't get out of here fast enough."

"Yeah, but I'm worse this time, Mother. They have to protect themselves or they couldn't stay on the floor. Their hurryin' by me is a sign that they care."

"They don't rush in and out when John's here."

"Well, they're only human, Mother," Peg giggled, "especially on Friday nights."

John always visited on Friday nights before he went down the street to Severence Hall to sing with the Cleveland Orchestra Chorus—in his tux.

Angie, of course, never rushed in and out, even when she was stationed at the other end of the hall and just dropped in to give Peg a back rub or keep her abreast of her life. "I'm reading *Jo's Boys*, Peg, working through the *Little Women* series. It's so fun!" Angie was as mature as a twenty-five-year-old woman could be, but the fun-light that shone on her face lifted the heaviness from us all.

"Angie's not backing off, Peggie."

"No, not Angie."

One day the guy-who-lived-with-Jillian-down-the-hall brought Peg a basket of red-ripe strawberries, but I had no knife to cut them with till Angie swished in the next morning with a paring knife still in its cardboard. "I was walking down the hill on my way here, Mrs. Woodson, and there it was plunk in the middle of the street."

On Mother's Day Peg presented me with a card she'd gotten on one of our wheels down to the gift shop, but with a present as well—a battery-run reading light with a hook attached to fasten to my book at night. "Angie found it, Mother."

"But how did you find something so unusual and exactly what I need?"

"Oh, I was walking down the hill on my way here," she beamed, "and there it was plunk in the middle of the street."

I yawned, hopped into my cot as though it were bedtime, clipped my light to my book, and knowing how Angie was struggling to determine what God wanted her to do next with her life, said, "Here, Angie, this quote is for you: 'You are seeking for secret ways of belonging to God, but there is only one: making use of whatever He offers you.' "

And then, as though I were finishing the quotation, I added, "Particularly when He offers it to you in the middle of your ordinary way."

Angie and Peggie both looked at me suspiciously, but all they said was, "Mmmmm."

John presented me with a pot of mums on Mother's Day with a card *for a special friend,* and when the strap on my watch broke, he took it home for his father to fix, and when his father couldn't fix it—what else—he bought me a new watch.

When I could no longer have an adult-to-young-adult-daughter relationship, could I still have adult-to-young-adult relationships? I could.

On my birthday, at the end of the first three weeks, Angie waltzed in with a box of decorated homemade cupcakes. "I was walking down the hill on my way here—"

"—and there they were plunk in the middle of the street," Peg and John and Joanne and I chorused.

I walked up and down *my street* that night passing out cupcakes to patients and parents and nurses.

Only Peg knew how hard that was for me to do. "I'm impressed, Mother."

◇　　◇　　◇

Did you know that John and Angie have spent every eve-before-Christmas-Eve since you died with your father and me? Or that Angie had lunch with me every week for a year after your death? She went off then to study for her master's. She's working in Virginia now as a nurse practitioner—and reading through the Anne of Green Gables *series. John's work as a producer brings him to a studio near my office on Tuesday mornings, and he spends Tuesday afternoons in my office with me. And he takes your father and me out on our anniversary. You left me some kind of a legacy in your friends as well as your families, Peggie.*

◇ ◇ ◇

Friends from the church came during those two and a half weeks and hauled our dirty clothes to the laundry room at Ronald MacDonald House. It felt a little bit like *hanging out your dirty wash* must feel, but it also felt like the most personal love-in-action.

And one of my writer friends exulted in her unemployment because it meant she could take me to get my driver's license renewed, while another writer friend arrived with a quart of fried rice from the Fiery Dragon for Peg.

"The only restaurant in Cleveland that makes fried rice I like, Mother, with pork and egg in it. How could she know?"

And Jan left her sculpturing and came, just to be with me. Jan's four-month-old son had died in this hospital four years before, and with her son, her faith. But then she read the book I had written about my son's death in this hospital, and we became friends, and in time Jan's faith came back to life.

Jan's mother died during Peg's six weeks in the hospital, but Jan kept coming with Care Bears for Peggie and excursions for me to Greek and kosher restaurants up beyond Little Italy. After Peggie's death, she became inoperable for a while, but not while I needed her.

"You have no idea, Meg," Jan said, "how unusual it is for you to be going through what you're going through and not once question God."

"I've lived with C.F. and with God for a long time, Jan. You should have known me twenty years ago."

"It's still unusual. I can't tell you how it reinforces me."

I let myself be reinforced by my reinforcement of my friend. I let my soul as well as my body be fed by a bite now and then of fried rice from the Fiery Dragon.

Yes, my friends had been my friends before, but they moved in in a new way now, and I welcomed them in.

Though, of course, the love from that period that still

vibrates most preciously on every ragged string of my heart is the love that thrummed between Peggie and me as we talked and laughed alone together.

"Ya know those six weeks I lived in the hospital with Marilyn, Mother? Well, they gave Marilyn a trache, and every day she went downstairs and they put antibiotics through the trache directly into her lungs. I mean, that was hard for me to watch because she made these gurgling noises, but it meant a lot for her to have me there, so it meant a lot for me to be there. Do you understand what I mean?

"It was strange with Marilyn, but after she died, I sat in my apartment and cried and thought, *I'll never visit her in the hospital again. She'll never call me on the phone again. I'll never again go to Washington and sit in front of the fireplace with Marilyn and her cats.* I mean, I cried a lot, and you know me, I only let myself fall apart once when a C.F. friend dies or I'd be crying all the time.

"Everybody was so nice to me when I lived in the hospital with Marilyn. Like only parents are allowed to stay overnight, but they gave me a fold-down chair to sleep on, and if they had time, the nurses did my therapy. I was so proud that Dr. Rathburn called me to come, though I don't think he intended me to stay. I look back on those six weeks as the worst and the best of my life. Do you understand what I'm saying, Mother?"

◊   ◊   ◊

I understand more now than I did at the time, Peggie. Ben says, based on all I've told him about you, that while you were exceptionally mature in some ways, you were immature emotionally . . . about sixteen. Don't yell, don't yell. Remember where you are!

He says that a lot of people remain adolescents emotionally till their late twenties, and that with you it might have happened because the taunts of the kids at school and the deaths of your C.F. friends and your own sickening were more than you could handle. You got stuck emotionally in teenagery, and to your father's and my misfortune, you died before you got unstuck. Ben says that your altogether accepting people or altogether writing them off is typical adolescent behavior, that only when a young person matures enough to accept her own limitations is she able to accept the limitations of others. I keep reminding your father of that.

And I understand, Peggie, that when you took care of Marilyn, for the first time in your maiden life, you experienced yourself as unable to deal perfectly with a situation, and that in telling me about it, you may have been lifting your condemnation of me for getting distraught over you.

Wouldn't it have been wonderful, Peggie, if you could have grown up all the way on earth? Oh, Peggie, what would you have become? And what on earth—what in heaven— are you like now?

◇　◇　◇

"I understand, Peggie, that I will always look back on this time I'm living in the hospital with you as the best time of my life because you want me here," I said, and cried. I cried in front of Peggie, and she cried back, and what a weight lifted.

And then she went into such a coughing fit that Angie ran in and stood on one side of the bed while I stood on the other. And when the coughing subsided, Peggie said to Angie, "Isn't my mother doin' good?"

I walked casually from the room and then ran pell-mell down the hall to cry in the Parents Lounge so Peg wouldn't cry again, cough again. *Did you hear what she said, God? Peggie—my Peggie—thinks her mother's doin' good.*

◇　◇　◇

"You remember how upset I got when I graduated from college, Mother, and nobody would hire me as a full-time editor because of my C.F.? I mean, nobody would hire me as a part-time editor. Nobody would hire me part time as a file clerk. But did I ever tell you how I went waterskiing when I lived with Elaine's family during that time?

"Well, waterskiing was one of the most fun things I ever

did. I'm not sayin' it made up for nobody hiring me, but the third day I tried to waterski, I stayed up for five seconds. Yah! I was thinking so hard about hanging on to the rope and not killing myself, I forgot I had C.F.

"After waterskiing Poopa always took us out for steaks, even though it made Mooma mad. I felt like I belonged to that family too, the way they argued right in front of me.

"And John invited me to spend Labor Day with his family, and there are so many of them and they're so close-knit, they don't ask anybody but family for holidays. Did I tell you I finally got all John's sisters and his brother straight in my head, and their spouses and kids? Like Kathleen is married to Mike O'Shaunessey, and they have four kids, Megan and—here, let me draw you a family tree."

Families-schamilies. Still, I wanted nothing more than to sit in my lawn chair by Peg's bed and have her confide in me, Mooma and Poopa notwithstanding.

"Dr. Rathburn is talkin' about giving me MucoMist," she hissed in the night, "but one of the dippy nurses told me it can thin the mucus in your lungs so much you drown in it or go into heart failure."

She became obsessed at night with med schedules and with her broviac. "The last time I was in, Mother, this nurse hooked up an I.V. to my broviac and then forgot me and went off duty, and a blood clot formed—at midnight. I mean, they suctioned it out, but what if I hadn't woke up and found it? That's when I bought my little alarm clock. But I shouldn't have to wake myself up all night to see that the nurses are doing their job. Can't you pull your chair up any closer to me, Mother?"

As meticulous in their care of Peg as the night nurses were, they failed to meet the standards of *la grande dame sans merci*, and she punctuated her rantings in the dark with "Oh, brother!" and "And this is the best there is!"

Still, she ranted only to me.

One midday when the sun was bright in the sky and we could feel its strength on our skin through the window, I asked Peg if she had any idea why things seemed so black at midnight.

And Joanne piped in, "Oh, that's because when you sleep you don't control your breathing like you do when you're awake, and it's more shallow, and you don't get enough oxygen, and the first thing that happens when you don't get enough oxygen is that you get upset."

Peg and I gaped at our newfound authority on nighttime anxiety attacks.

"I know," Joanne grinned, "because it's like that with asthma, too. Once you know why you get upset, you still get upset, but it doesn't bother you as much, and you know you'll feel better in the morning."

"Why did we have to wait for Joanne to tell us that?" Peg hissed in the night. "We'd get so much less hyper about stuff if we knew what to expect."

No matter. We were alone, the daughter lying in her hospital bed hissing at the mother hugging the daughter's bed, the only mother-daughter stars lit in a dark-domed galaxy.

◊   ◊   ◊

A lot of things we talked about in those days were things that made us laugh.

"Remember when I brought Marilyn's Scoota back with me from my second trip to Washington, Mother? Well, I was scootin' all over Cleveland-Hopkins Airport on that thing, and then we got in this tiny elevator to get down to baggage claim, and Jody and John and I were packed in there with the Scoota, but we managed to get it turned around so I could ride it out, and then the elevator opened on the other side, and we were going up and down in the elevator, I mean up and down and up and down, before we finally got out, and we were laughin' so hard, everybody was looking at us like we were on something."

"You know how most of the nurses have never heard of the allergy pills you take, Peggie? Well, one of them asked Angie if they were birth control pills."

"What?" Peg whooped. "What? What?"

"And Angie said, 'No, they're not birth control pills.' "

"And the first nurse said, 'Well, what about the guy who

comes to see her in the tux?' "

"Oh, no, I can't believe it," Peg moaned in glee, disbelieving that anyone would think she took birth control pills, let alone for John. Yet she was careful not to laugh as she had laughed in the old days.

When I think of our laughter times in those two and a half weeks in the hospital, I see Peg lying flat in her bed, arms to her sides holding her body stiff, not letting her body laugh, but laughter bursting forth nonetheless through her wide-mouthed grin.

"Nobody could get in the Parents Lounge this afternoon, Peg, and finally maintenance opened the door, and Mrs. Canfield had gone in there to read and fell asleep."

Peg's body stiffened and her face split. "Ha ha!" Strange how some things that weren't all that funny seemed hilarious at the time.

◊ ◊ ◊

I'm reading The State of Stony Lonesome, *Peg, by Jessamyn West. The girl in the book calls her mother Birdeen and says: "Birdeen could make me laugh. No hugging, no kissing. No reading of stories aloud. . . . But the laughing together was a mingling, maybe closer than hugging and kissing; a hugger or kisser in many cases might as well have been embracing stone. But the laughter of two laughees really mingles and makes the two one."*

I've not forgotten, Peg, the day you came home from your apartment, stood inside the front door listening, and said, "This is a sad house." Sometimes you said, "This is a tense house." That was for your father. But when you said, "This is a sad house," that was for me. I laugh so much more now than I used to, you wouldn't know me. I wish I could be the better mother I would be to you now, Peg—and my kingdom for a granddaughter. I would not make the mistakes with a granddaughter I made with you.

Wasn't it wonderful in the hospital, Peg, the way the laughter of us two laughees mingled us! One of the things I miss most is talking to you about what I've been reading, but the thing I miss most of all is laughing with my daughter about anything at all.

I was in the bathroom this morning, Peggie, brushing my teeth, and your father was serenading me from outside the door with what he considered a love song, only it was "Desert Song," something a sheik would sing to a member of his harem. Now your father knows that I hate songs like that, so I waited till his voice reached its most fervent pitch—and flushed the toilet. Ha ha. That was a funny thing, wasn't it, Peggie? Oh, ha ha.

◊   ◊   ◊

Sometimes things were thrust upon us that weren't funny at all but that we had to laugh about to live with, like when Lucella moved into Karol's bed. Lucella had radio, TV, and stereo, and she played all three at top decibels, simultaneously, while talking on the phone.

"Now maybe you understand what a hospital room is usually like, Mother."

Lucella had stumps for arms and was retarded, and we all felt for her, but try as we would to make her a part of the room, she'd have nothing to do with us.

Then we noticed a sign on the door to our room, complete with skull and crossbones: WARNING! INFECTIOUS HEPATITIS. DO NOT ENTER!

"Lucella has infectious hepatitis, Angie?" Mrs. Canfield.

"Yes."

"Well, why isn't she in one of the isolation rooms?" Peggie.

"Well, she would be, but they're both full."

"What?" Joanne and Mandy.

"Oh, it's okay. You can only catch it through contact with blood or urine. That's why she has a potty chair beside her bed."

"So why, when Sandy changes her bed, does she wear a gown over her uniform and rubber gloves?" Me.

"Well, some people are super-cautious."

We all flopped back in nervous laughter, and we all became super-cautious, especially Peg, whose eagle eyes caught Lucella going into our bathroom at two o'clock one morning and not coming out.

Lucella told the nurse, summoned by Peggie, that she had gone in the bathroom to change her clothes. But in the middle of the night? Why hadn't she pulled the curtain around her bed to change her clothes? And how long could changing your clothes take?

What was Lucella doing in the bathroom? became the scared-giggle. It was to our credit that Lucella never knew how uneasily we giggled over her.

◊   ◊   ◊

Of course, I could not have taken the pleasure I did in my growing closeness to Peg had not Peg begun to draw her father close to her. She never mentioned why she drew him close. She never mentioned that she drew him close, but draw her father close she did.

◊   ◊   ◊

Oh, Peggie. Bless you, bless you, Peggie!

◊   ◊   ◊

Like the Sunday afternoon he came over and invited everyone in the room to join in devotions—if they liked. Then when he'd given a synopsis of his sermon from that morning and had a prayer for everyone, Peg said, "Now that we've had this much, we may as well have the whole service. How about the benediction, Father?"

And Joe put his hand on her head and pronounced the benediction that since her girlhood had made her feel that *God is up there lookin' over me:* "The Lord bless thee and keep thee. The Lord make His face to shine upon thee. The Lord lift up His countenance upon thee and give thee peace."

Joe's condensation of his sermon centered around the Twenty-third Psalm: *The Lord is my Shepherd; I shall not want.*

"God is with us in the good times," he said, "and God is with us in the bad times. Even when we walk through the valley of the shadow of death, we don't need to be afraid because Jesus is our Shepherd."

Peg kind of cried when she asked for the benediction, because, as she put it to me later, "Every time in my whole life when Father has said, 'The Lord give thee peace,' the Lord has given me peace, and ya know, it's the strangest thing, but every time in my whole life when Father has said, 'Yea, though I walk through the valley of the shadow of death, I will fear no evil,' the Lord has given me the exact same feeling—and you can tell Father that if you want to."

I told him, and that was all Joe had to hear. Over and over throughout the rest of Peg's hospitalization, he read the Twenty-third Psalm to her and pronounced the benediction over her.

"I hope Father doesn't feel bad that we talk the way we do, Mother. His prayers are his important thing, even when they're repetitious. I mean, he has this knack of always saying the right thing—and you can tell him that too, if you want to."

"I don't think you have any idea, Joe, how much Peg looks to you for spiritual guidance. I get jealous sometimes because I work at fostering her relationship with God too, but all through the years, you're the one she's credited with bringing God to her."

"How do you know God is with you when you can't feel Him?" Peg asked her father toward the end of our first three weeks in the hospital as her cough and her weakness worsened.

And Joe told her about the time when she was newborn and he took her out and it began to rain and he held her under his raincoat in the crook of his arm, where she fit exactly. "You were sleeping, Peggie. You didn't know I was carrying you, but your not knowing didn't make a particle of difference. I was still sheltering you from the rain."

Joe was sitting beside Peg with his hand on her bed, being careful not to move it toward her, when Peg walked her fingers over her dusky-pink butterfly sheet and tapped his hand a time or two with her middle finger.

And a tear slid down Joe's cheek, and his voice shook as

he said, "God is our Father, Peg, and He loves us far more than any earthly father loves his daughter, and He's holding you all the time, especially when you need Him most, especially when you can't feel Him."

After Joe left, Peg asked me to read to her out of my book, and I read, with a touch of condemnation in my voice for sins she had visited on her father in the past, but mostly with commendation for the work of the present day, "Let us love, for love will give us everything."

"Come on, Mother," Peg scorned. "I'm on to you making some of that stuff up. Read to me what's really there."

"Well, give me a minute, Peggie—these things don't always leap off the page at me."

Then, when I knew I'd found the right selection, I brought the book over to her and pointed as I read: "Jesus . . . has shown me the only path which leads to the divine . . . love. It is the complete abandonment of a baby sleeping without fear in its father's arms. . . ."

"Auk!"

"And here's another one, Peg, not just for today but for all our days," and I pointed again as I read again: "Let us love, for love will give us everything."

◊   ◊   ◊

I can't tell you, Peggie, how many times since your death your father has sat hunched over, voice choking with despair as he says, "I have to admit that there were a number of years when Peggie pretty much put me out of her life." But then he stretches his neck up like a rooster greeting a new day and, head high, he crows, "But I got her back in the hospital." Over and over. "I got her back in the hospital."

And all those new days dawn with glory, Peg. Glory.

11

I don't know why I think of May 17 as the end of the casual-slide period of Peg's hospitalization.

Perhaps because it was three weeks since I'd taken up residence in the hospital and would be another three weeks, less one day, before I gave up residence.

Perhaps because May 17th was my birthday. A childish consideration, but I dragged through the day in solemn awareness that I would never celebrate another birthday with a child of mine, that no celebration would count in the same way again.

Perhaps because I woke that morning not only to the sight of Peg slumped over her bed tray, but to the sound of her groaning. Peg was not a groaner, but her headache that morning bypassed her and pounded out its own audible protest. She'd been waking up each morning with minor headaches, but this morning she contracted her mouth muscles when she spoke so as not to intensify the pain in her head by the slightest facial movement. "Mary—already gave me—Tylenol—but it—hasn't helped."

Only time eased these early morning headaches, and an hour or two eased even this one, but then she said—Peggie Woodson asked—"Will you wash my hair today, Mother?"

And I did.

John arrived just as I finished and looked aghast at Peg's can't-talk-right-now exhaustion.

Dear God, if she can't rally for John, can she rally? How did this happen so quickly? The *knowing* I'd pushed into the back of my mind for two and a half weeks blared back into full consciousness in the front of my own pounding head.

An orderly carted Peg off to X-ray collapsed over a pillow in her wheelchair, orderlies not given to coming back later when patients feel up to going to X-ray.

John looked, stricken, at Peggie's empty bed. "I've known Peggie since the ninth grade," he said, and sensing that he needed to talk, I asked how it had come about, though I knew the story well.

"Well, Peggie was sitting in front of me in Advanced English talking about a book her mother had written about her. I'd never known anybody whose mother had written a book about them, so I got my mother to buy me a copy, figuring it was an Erma Bombeck mother-daughter type book!

"Then when I got into it . . . well, I stayed in my room all weekend reading and crying. Sometimes I've asked myself why I didn't back off right then, but once I got to know Peggie, I sort of forgot about the death thing. Some perky girls are a pain, but Peggie was naturally perky, and smart too. That's another thing I remember from those days—how studious she looked in class.

"It's interesting to look back on junior high and high school, because while Peg and I rejected what a lot of kids were doing with sex and drugs, it didn't mean we couldn't have a good time. Like once we were talking on the phone, and I whipped out the yellow pages and proceeded to read them to her. We laughed for an hour over the crazy things people advertised and never got past the A's.

"That's how it's always been with us. We have a good time doing nothing, just being together." And a desperation in John's voice added, *And that's how it always will be.*

"Another important thing about back then is that we built each other up. Like Peggie was always telling me how great my music was and how good-lookin' I was. Nobody else ever outright told me those things. . . ."

And then, as Peg was wheeled back into the room, he

added, "And she always said, 'And don't you forget, John Patrick Byrne, that I have approval rights over any girl you get serious with.' "

"And don't you forget, John Patrick Byrne, I still do," Peg panted in the best imitation she could manage of his imitation of her high-pitched, teacherish tones.

That was the first day John cut classes to stay with Peggie, and when I walked him to the elevator, he said, "I still think Peggie's going to be all right, and I still think Peggie thinks she's going to be all right . . . so why do I feel disloyal to her for talking to you about her?" And he slung his arm across my shoulders.

Where had he come from, this magnificent young man, to be with us here? And where would he go from here? *He's hurting, God. Don't let him be harmed, God—but helped here. Let him go from here to a very good place.*

I followed Dr. Rathburn into the hall without subterfuge that day. "Peggie is getting worse fast."

"She's on the three antibiotics that have always done it for her."

"But it's as though she's on nothing."

"She's not responsive to anything else."

"What about ceftazadime?" I pressed, referring to an experimental drug the patients talked about with reverence. But the doctor said they had ceftazadime in such limited quantities that they had to save it for patients with cepatia, and then as a last resort.

"So there's nothing you—" How could there be nothing?

◊　　◊　　◊

"Will you ask Jan to pray about something, *Ma*?" Peg asked that night, convinced on good evidence that Jan's prayers got through as few people's did. "Now I'm gonna cry, so don't pay any attention. Okay, here's the thing. If I'm going to keep on feeling this crummy, I'd like to know that I'm putting the glory around it, and I don't know for sure, so will you ask Jan to pray that I'll know? . . . I mean, I'm trying to give it a glory by being the best possible patient, but maybe I'm just tough. I need to know."

Where had she come from? Who had formed this feeble young woman who sat there on the edge of her bed summoning the initiative to take a few faltering steps to the bathroom—and worrying about fulfilling her destiny?

Thank You, God, that Peg is going from here to the best of places. I'm getting really tired, God. I don't know how long I can handle all this. I couldn't handle it, Father, if I didn't know that on the other side Your Glory is waiting for Peg.

"Don't you see, Peggie, that your wanting to turn this hard time into glory is a glory in itself?"

"But even if I know I'm doin' it, how will anybody else know? Maybe they'll think I'm just naturally a good patient."

I told her that God would know, and the angels, and that her father and I and John and Angie and everybody who truly knew her would know.

"But how, Mother? How will they know?"

"There are monks, Peggie, who spend their lives shut away in monasteries praying. Do you think their lives glorify God even when nobody knows what they're doing, even when nobody knows that they're there?"

"Leave it to my mother to ask a question I can't answer. . . . Is Father coming tonight? He is? Is Father coming tomorrow?"

And that's why I think of May 17 as the end of the first period of Peg's hospitalization . . . because John was admitting to much amiss, because Dr. Rathburn was admitting to much amiss, and because Peg was admitting not only to much pain but to urgent longing to be bright and beautiful for God.

On May 17 the casual slide became a cataclysm. Oh, yes.

◇   ◇   ◇

A mother and a C.F. daughter came from Kansas to Cleveland last week, Peg, to see Dr. Rathburn. A mutual friend asked me to drive them from the airport to the hospital, and I did. Oh, yes.

I walked with the mother and daughter from the parking garage through the underground tunnels in the route I walked so many times with you. Got lost with them trying to find Pediatric X-ray, as we got lost so many times together trying to find Pediatric X-ray.

"I feel like I should track you down and ply you with questions," I said that to Dr. Rathburn, "but there are no more questions to ask." Cry, cry, the beloved daughter.

I didn't go up to the fourth floor. I hadn't the courage for that.

Once, though, when the mother and daughter were in Dr. Rathburn's office, I dashed to the cafeteria, looked in at the vending machines. Ran on down to the corridor with the bulletin boards. Couldn't find a funny thing.

I guess I'm thinking about the day I went back to the hospital now as I'm writing about May 17 because in a way there weren't any questions to ask from that day on, and . . . I don't know, Peggie, because they were both such awful days of such awful truth.

◇   ◇   ◇

"Could you move your cot right up to my bed, Mother, so you can keep your hand on my leg through the night?" Peg asked as that long day came to an end. "It's good to have you here, Mother."

My cot was lower than Peg's bed, but I managed to keep my hand up there till she drifted off to sleep, and even then I anchored my hand to Peggie's leg, my hand and my arm and my spirit numb.

12

"*D*id Joey suffer much?" people asked after his death.

"Well, he was just so tired, and he had a hard time breathing." It didn't sound like much, but it had been more than a twelve-year-old son could live with.

And it was worse for Peggie, even during the first five days of the second half of her hospitalization as she plummeted into dire tiredness, into rougher coughing, into more toilsome breathing than a twenty-three-year-old daughter could live with, but did.

She didn't wake me at night anymore, though her breathing became more shallow and though I willed her to wake me. Perhaps increasing lack of oxygen dulled her brain till she could not waken, not till the blast of pain in her head shot her up from the pillows on her bed and over onto the pillow I now fit each night into that amazing, expanding array of supplies on her bed tray.

And that was when she woke me now, at five or five-thirty in the morning, when she could no longer stand alone, slump alone, against the pain in her head. How long she lay there with her head detonating before waking me, I did not know, but her disintegration when I got to her was such that I knew it had been long.

Dr. Rathburn suspected that Peg's headaches resulted from the massive doses of collistin she was taking, the antibiotic always the most effective for her, and he offered to take her off it, but Peg would not give up on her last, best hope of recovery.

Good. Oh, good. I didn't want her head to keep hurting, but if she gave up, she'd no longer be Peggie—Peggie would no longer be.

Three pictures from the five days of Peg's *first dive* period fixed themselves in my mind.

The first was of Peggie collapsed over her pillow before even the day had rubbed the night from its eyes, moist from the drain of pain, limp from the pain of pain, with me sitting beside her, a sweaty, doubled-over hump of my pain for her.

The second was of Peggie in her wheelchair in the tub room. "My wheelchair won't fit under the sink in my room, Mother, but in the tub room there's a spray, and I can stay in my wheelchair and on my oxygen and lean over the tub while you wash my hair."

Late every morning when the pain in Peg's head abated, I took a basin and in it collected shampoo and conditioner, hospital pajama bottoms in which she was now more comfortable than in her cords, T-shirt, three towels, washcloth, socks, underpants, tissues, soap, deodorant, mucus cup.

Then I transferred her oxygen cannula from the oxygen supply above her bed to the oxygen tank on her wheelchair—*Please, God, keep me calm*—helped her into her wheelchair and pushed her down to the overheated tub room. The mechanics of the simplest of tasks exhausted us both.

The sicker Peg got, the more any inefficiency on my part unsettled her, so my second picture of her, in her wheelchair in the tub room, focused on her sorting through the supplies in the basin on her lap, sure I'd forgotten something and keeping at it till she discovered what it was.

I could see she was wearing herself out holding in her rage, so I told her to feel free to yell.

And she yelled, "Well, honestly, Mother, you forgot my socks. Yesterday the deodorant, today the socks, and tomorrow who knows what? It is beyond me how you always manage to forget something. And don't think I don't know how upset you get bringing me down here. It is beyond me how you manage to get upset about every little thing."

"And it is beyond me," I yelled, "how you manage to be so picky about every little thing."

She didn't say anything then, but the next day when she had navigated from bed to wheelchair and I put the basin in her lap, she said, "I just want to say one thing, Mother. You told me it was all right for me to get angry at you, that we were on top of each other all the time and I was under a lot of stress and you would understand, but when I got angry, you got angry back. That wasn't fair."

I agreed that it wasn't fair, told her I was sorry and would do my best not to yell at her again, but that I was under a lot of stress, too, and I hoped she'd understand if I lost control sometimes too.

But, then, neither of us lost control again—in front of each other—though I wished Peggie would. Still, I knew I would never forget how she looked in the tub room, with barely the strength to sit in her wheelchair, bent over the basin in her lap examining the fly on her unisex pajama bottoms making sure I had fastened the fly shut with five safety pins, of the same size, going in the same direction, equidistant apart.

It didn't help to have Mrs. Canfield and Mandy being the model mother and daughter. How often I'd been torn in my life between being a writer and a mother, while Mrs. Canfield, I could tell, had never wanted to be anything but Mandy's mother.

It became harder and harder to get Peg comfortable at night. She couldn't breathe lying flat or even on an incline, so we collected extra hospital pillows, and Joe brought in two fluffy ones from home, and we put one of the sides on her bed up and arranged the pillows in that corner so she could lean back against them and be all but upright. For some reason she flung her arms straight out to her sides when she reclined on her pillows. We called it her Cleopatra pose.

"On the fifth floor they have crushed ice instead of ice

cubes, Mother," she proclaimed in feeble yet royal tones. "I prefer my ice crushed, so kindly fetch my ice from five from this night forward." She gave her arms an extra "ta-ta" fling to her sides, and that was the third picture of Peggie I would never forget—Peggie as Cleopatra-to-the-hilt.

I scuttled off to fetch her ice from five. She was my sovereign.

Peg was less tired at bedtime than at any other time, but still . . . to need so many pillows to hold her up. To reach into the last of her resources to ham it up.

"People don't realize that being so tired you can't roll over is like pain," I said to Dr. Rathburn.

"People don't realize that drawing for every breath is like pain," he replied. We'd had the same exchange over Joey.

How it hurt to look at these pictures of Peggie: Peggie hurting and hot, Peggie tired and mad, Peggie tired yet *her majesty*. How could anyone so young look so old?

The worst were the Cleopatra pictures because so much of the old Peg was in them, and the old Peg was disappearing fast. Every day her head ached more fiercely than it had the day before. Every day she was, impossibly, more tired. How much further down could she fall?

I'd heard somewhere that tension registers first in your eyes. I believed it, for my eyes hurt so as I looked at the pictures of Peg it seemed that the only thing keeping them from bursting were the multi-colored transparencies from another world that superimposed themselves upon the black-and-white scenes of this world and enabled me to keep on looking.

Like the zomax picture. All pain relievers available that might have reduced the pain in Peg's head also reduced respiration and were thus forbidden to her. Zomax, a prescription drug, didn't reduce respiration and had been the most effective pain reliever for Peg, but a few people had been allergic to it and the government had taken it off the market.

"It's bad enough to watch someone you love hurting when you know that nothing can help," I fumed to Jan, "but it's worse when you know that something can help and you can't get your hands on it."

Well, Jan had known a young man who had died of C.F. not long before—Terry Turner. Peg had been in the hospital when he died, though she did not know him well. Jan also knew Terry's mother. "Did Terry use zomax, Mrs. Turner," she asked, "and do you have any left by chance?"

Well, Terry's mother had given all his drugs to the C.F. Pharmacy to give to some other C.F. family but had not included his zomax, and, she said, she would be overjoyed if her Terry's zomax could help my Peggie. So Jan arrived the next day spilling out the serendipitous story and surreptitiously palming a bottle of zomax to Peg.

"By chance, eh?" Peg gloated, clutching the bottle to her Star Trek T-Shirt.

After that when I fixed Peg's bed tray at night, I added a third mucus cup, set in its lid, and concealed between the cup and the lid so many zomax to be taken as the night progressed. And a pencil and pad "so I can keep a record of when I take them, Mother, in case I get groggy and forget."

In the mornings when she could no longer lift her head to find the pills, I staggered to the kitchen for fresh water, placed a zomax in her mouth, and positioned a straw so she could swallow the pill without the tiniest movement of her head, the rest of her body giving the tiniest sigh of satisfaction.

As I sat with Peggie at these times, I remembered my own headaches, migraines. I'd tolerate them for as long as I could and then crawl to wherever Joe was. "I can't stand this pain, Joe."

Sometimes he'd massage the space over my eyes. Sometimes he'd press my head to his face. Neither took away the pain in my head, though rubbing my eyes helped, but when pain hammers that hard at your body, it batters your spirit too, and any sign of love toward the outer part rests you within.

"God's awake at five o'clock in the morning, isn't He, Mother?" Peg asked as her zomax mornings wore on.

And He was. God placing the zomax in Peg's mouth; God

ever so lightly pressing her cheek to His; Peg giving a wee sigh of acceptance. Our first other-world picture.

The zomax didn't take away the pain in Peg's head, but it relieved it enough so she could keep on with the collistin.

None of us involved in Peg's plunge accused God of not being there for us—how could we?—not, at least, until all hospital pictures had been painted and were long dry.

◇　◇　◇

Yet people were supposed to die slowly . . . slowly. People had to die slowly because other people had to have time to get ready.

And why was it necessary for me to pin down what happened on the second day or on the third night of Peg's hospitalization? Well, any record of events that momentous had to be kept straight. But, also, any events that unmanageable had somehow to be *managed*—like the events of the first five days of the second half of Peggie's last hospitalization.

Joanne kept a diary, and I asked her to copy out for me any entries she had made about Peg that she wouldn't mind my seeing. She couldn't scribble the entries out fast enough:

> 4/27—Day I came in. Peggie pretty sick. 4/28—Peggie coughing and coughing. 5/4—Peggie is really scaring me with how sick she is getting. 5/5—Peggie is a little better, not much. 5/6—Peggie got sick this morning with headaches but got better as the day wore on. 5/8—Peggie still can't talk but is doing better.

But all those entries were dated during the first two and a half weeks of Peg's hospitalization when I convinced myself she was doing well. While I felt bad about what we were putting Joanne through, I was touched by her recognition of what was happening to Peg and by the simple realness of her feelings. Though I suspected, from when her entries about Peg ended, that even Joanne could not look full-on at what was happening to Peggie now.

◇　◇　◇

One day when Lucella had gone home and Joanne was wandering the wards, Mrs. Canfield raised her voice at Mandy—unheard of. Peg and I stared across the room at Mrs. Canfield glaring down at Mandy—unbelievable. "Well, I'm doing the best job I can!" the angel mother spat.

And the angel child spat right back at her, "Well, it's not good enough!"

I pulled the curtain around Peg's bed so they'd not see us hug ourselves in glee or hear Peg's whisper: "Them, too! Did you hear that? Them, too!"

And then Ned, Peg's favorite member of our church, came to see her and left a book for me, *Three Came Home* by Agnes Newton Keith, the only book I read during my six weeks in the hospital besides my handbook. And every time I picked it up, I wondered why I was weighing myself down with the saga of a group of women shuttled from prison camp to prison camp by the Japanese during World War II.

Perhaps I persisted because it was a strength-of-the-human-spirit saga, and as I trudged with this group of faltering humans from camp to camp, enduring with them hunger and thirst and fever and swollen, blistered feet, refusing with them to fall into ditch or disintegration, my spirit too grew strong. Yet how I exhausted myself on those forced marches. How I cringed from the rats in the barracks and the maggots in the gruel.

Ned had marked a passage in the book he thought I'd like in which the author compared the secular women with whom she lived in one camp with a group of Catholic sisters interned there. I copied the passage out on a paper towel:

> They formed in general a background of prayer and peace, for the rest of our world which was mad. The thing that struck me first of all was that the sisters were happy; next, resourceful; third, they were holy; and finally they, like ourselves, *could sometimes be hysterical*. (italics mine)

Them too! I exulted night after night on my cot as I beamed my book light on this passage.

Most mothers and daughters would not have been as upset as Peg and I over one angry exchange in a tub room, but . . . why couldn't this mother use her last opportunity to make up for past sins visited on her daughter? And why couldn't this daughter create only memories of love for her mother?

God didn't care why. *Be human, Peg,* He said through the brashly lighted picture of the Madonna and child across the room. *Be real, Meg,* He said through the crazily slanted picture of the brides of Christ in far-off Malaysia. *Go easy on yourselves, my children.*

Then there was the night John brought in a stereo system—tape deck, speakers, earphones—so Peg could enjoy her music on something more sumptuous than her tiny tape recorder. Somehow he rearranged the items on the game table and set up the stereo there, every gesture of his muscular body crying: *For Peggie.*

When Peg was ready to go to sleep, he put John Michael Talbot's "The Last Supper" on the stereo and the earphones on Peg's head.

"But the earphones are so heavy, John. I won't have the strength to take them off."

"I'll sit with you till you're asleep, Peg, and take the earphones off for you."

A simple exchange, one I wouldn't have heard had I not been walking past Peg's bed at the time—walking on holy ground.

John sat with Peggie, playing tape after tape, till midnight. I knew because I was in my cot, desperate to go to the bathroom but too self-conscious to get up in my nightgown in front of this young man. So I kept looking over to see if he was still there, and he was, and he was, sitting in the dark and the quiet looking down on Peggie.

All I could see was his back, but the next day, Peggie said, "You know last night when John was sitting on my bed? Well, there was this look on his face like he really loved me. Wasn't it nice of him to sit there? I saw such love in his face for me last night, and I felt the same love for him, and you can tell him that if you want to, Mother."

We got talking then about everybody having a most-cherished person in their lives, and I told Peggie she was mine, she looking away sheepishly, not being able to say the same to me.

"That's okay, honey. Usually a child is a mother's most-cherished person, but if the mother cherishes the child rightly, the child goes out and finds her own most-cherished person. That's the way love moves on. I think John is your most-cherished person, and I'm nothing but glad that you have him."

"Yes, John is my most-cherished person, Mother, and you can tell him that too, if you want to. Did you know that John means *gift of God*? I looked it up in the book of names when I was finding a name for my broviac."

And that's the many-splendored transparency through which I viewed Peg's night time, used-up-by-the-daytime Cleopatra pose—the love in John's eyes as he looked down on her till she slept, reflected in the love in Peggie's eyes for John.

As long as I lived I would be grateful that John was there for Peggie as long as she lived. Without John, hers would have been a different dying.

◊   ◊   ◊

Many things about Peg's dying were different from Joey's, but one thing stands out. With Joey, I hoped.

I believed. Joey would not die. Till the end I was Abraham on the mountain offering my son to God, sure that when my offering was complete, God would spare my *Isaac*. And even when Joey died—though I have not till this moment admitted it to anyone—I sat by his little grave and waited for a resurrection.

I might have hoped again, but *I could not*. Most people think it's always better to hope for life. Not so. I've lived through a child's death with hope and without hope, and if the child is going to die, it is better to live without hope. Please . . . I know.

So while I could not altogether keep from asking God to keep Peg from dying, how could I believe that Peg would be one of the rare miracle breed when the God-pictures kept saying, *I know it's hard, but I'm with you.* The outward assurances handed into our troubled time from the eternity of God's love were indications to me that Peg would die.

On the last of the five nights of her *descent*, she said, gasping for air, "Read—to me—Mother."

"How about something out of the Bible tonight, Peg?" I asked, and quoted to her verse thirty-three of the sixteenth chapter of the gospel of John: "I have told you these things, so that in me you may have peace. In this world you will have trouble. But take heart! I have overcome the world."

"Yeah—I like that—Mother. That—has the—ring of truth."

13

Somewhere in the middle of Peg's five-day plunge, Mary, the head nurse, asked, "Would you be more comfortable in a private room, Peggie?"

"No. If I'm in a private room, I'll just think about myself," Peg said. "Here there are people to watch and lots of comings and goings. Anyway, I love Mandy and Joanne too much to leave them."

I knew Peg was doing the best thing for herself, but was it best for Joanne and Mandy?

Sometimes Joanne sat on her bed and looked at Peggie's sickness with such sickness on her face that I asked if she'd like me to draw the curtain between them. She always said yes.

And how must Mandy feel? While Mandy wasn't getting worse, she wasn't getting better. How must she feel, knowing she would soon stagger after Peggie down such a steep, merciless path?

When Mary left, Peggie asked me to take two of her helium balloons and give one to Joanne and one to Mandy.

"Peggie wants you to have one of her balloons, Mandy, and she wants me to tell you that she likes having you for a roommate and that she's sorry she hasn't been able to talk to you more."

And Mandy, in white shorty gown, its yellow daisies framing her fresh-flower face, said, "Tell Peggie I like having her for a roommate too, and that I understand when she can't talk because I know what it's like to be sick too." And two tears spattered her petal-soft cheeks. Why was it that mothers' children expressed their feelings about each other so openly but gave their mothers so few clues about their feelings toward them?

Then Peg, having determined where she would stay and having done what she could for the inhabitants of her room, said, "I want to go back to my apartment."

I could not bear for her to look at me with such hope in her eyes. Or was it the beginning of no-hope? Or was it the tension that resulted from not knowing whether to hope or not to hope?

I don't suppose she could go back to her apartment for just a short spell, could she, God? She didn't get to say good-bye to her things there, and she loves her apartment more than any place on earth.

Did you see Mandy just now, God, her pansy face held so straight upon a wilting stalk? Did you hear how she and Peggie care about each other? How hard it will be on Mandy if Peggie dies. And what about us mothers? What will we do without our children? Without each others' children?

"Sometimes, Mother," Peg said, "when you want to swear, but you know you shouldn't, if you just say *Swear*, that helps."

Swear, swear, I mouthed, and the tension broke.

◇　◇　◇

When Joe visited in the afternoon, he quoted the words with which Christ comforted His friends before He left them for heaven: "I am going to prepare a place for you."

"You know how much you love your apartment, Peg, how you've fixed it up with butterflies and rainbows and smile faces so that it's an extension of you—your very own place? Well, Jesus has prepared a *place for you* in heaven, an *apartment* where, even more than in your apartment in Bunting, you will be at home."

"Auk! How do you do that, Father? How do you know what I'm thinking? How do you always say the right thing?

. . . How does he do that, Mother?"

"Beats me, Peg."

After that when Joe visited, in between reading the Twenty-third Psalm to her and pronouncing the benediction over her, he quoted Christ's "I am going to prepare *a place for you.*" Over and over.

And, over and over, in front of the elevator or in the cafeteria or by the front door or in the parking garage, he hung his head low. "It's so hard, Meg, to watch your daughter watch the process of her death."

I think Joe, in his way, had a harder time than I, having to leave Peggie and go back to an empty house. I'd left step-by-step directions for him on how to use the washer and dryer, but he had to call in a neighbor to help. A church member up the street grocery-shopped for him, and others invited him for dinner. But, still, it was not good for Joe to live alone.

When I'd lived in the hospital with Joey, my parents had come to take care of things at home, but my father was dead now and my mother blind. So often now it seemed that there was nothing to life but death and bodies gone darkly haywire. Nor did it help to tell myself that such feelings were normal at such times and that they would pass as they had passed, in time, after Joey's death.

The thing that helped Joe the most, I could tell, was not being alone anymore when he was with Peggie. Forming a frame around the other multi-colored pictures of those five days were a series of Joe-and-Peggie pictures: Joe sitting beside Peg reading the Bible to her; Peggie soaking up Joe's words. Joe sitting beside Peg quietly, holding her hand; Peggie soaking up Joe. Joe coming over early one morning and finding Peg crying because she'd coughed all night and hadn't been able to sleep; Joe rubbing Peggie's legs.

All those looks of heartbreak and happiness on Joe's face as Peg continued to welcome him into her life—they were the most resplendent pictures of all.

How quickly Peg fell in those five days, whizzing down past me so swiftly, my vision blurred. On oxygen all the time, on more oxygen all the time. Stumbling the few steps

125

from bed to bathroom, being supported the few steps from bed to bathroom, being supported from bed to potty chair beside her bed. Eating nothing for five days but fried rice from the Fiery Dragon—three times a day—bit by laborious bit of manna from the gods—twice a day. Asking me to write her checks for her, pay the rent on her apartment. "I sure don't want to lose my apartment, Mother."

Peg enjoyed keeping records, and she was so meticulous about her checkbook that it had been untouched by any hands but hers. It was no violation of privacy for either of us when I gave Peg a bath in the tub room, but when I opened her checkbook—I could hardly look.

"I think I'll wear a hospital top today, Mother. They're cooler than T-shirts, and I don't have to pull them over my head."

Please, Peggie, don't be all patient.

No more wheelchair excursions except to the tub room, and then, "It won't kill me to miss one day washing my hair, Mother." And then all day, "How does my hair look, Mother? Can I skip a day now and then?"

Peg had always washed her hair every day because, under the best of circumstances, she perspired profusely and saltily from her C.F. Now under the worst of circumstances, her hair looked more and more sticky as the day progressed, but I told her she was wise to take a break now and then— and went to the tub room alone and washed my face with my saltwater tears.

Yet Peg's light did not go out.

"Angie's havin' John over for supper again, Mother. Isn't that neat? I mean, I really want them to be friends."

Finally it dawned on me. Just in case neither of them was going to have her, she was giving them to each other. How Peg's face shone with the joy of giving John and Angie to each other.

And then Mrs. Canfield and Mandy came back from Severance Mall with a present for Peg all done up in a box: a nightshirt, lightweight and easy to get into.

"The blue is to match your eyes, Peggie," Mandy said, pausing in her wheelchair by Peg's bed to make sure she really, really liked her gift. How Peg's face shone with the joy of being given to. Every time she wore her blue, button-down-the-front, regular-person nightshirt, she waved to Mandy and pointed to the shirt and smiled.

And how Mandy's face shone as she smiled back across the room in acceptance of Peg's acceptance of her giving-ness.

◇   ◇   ◇

John spent more and more time at the hospital.

"Go, John," Peg nagged. "Get out of here. You have to graduate, remember?"

John insisted that with the courses he was taking, as long as he turned in his papers, his professors didn't care whether or not he was in class.

"Mmmm."

And Angie, if she worked the second shift, instead of going home at midnight, tiptoed in to see if Peg was awake. And Peg would be keeping herself awake for Angie, and they'd whisper best-friend confidences till two in the morning.

"Do you think she has a chance, Angie?"

"Well, I'm not sure."

Angie didn't hold out false hope, but she didn't take away hope either.

"Do you want to talk, Mrs. Woodson?" She didn't force herself on me but was available to me. "Are you ready for your Wednesday back rub? . . . Are you minding me and getting off the floor like I told you to?"

Later I learned that Angie lost fifteen pounds during the six weeks of Peggie's hospitalization.

◇   ◇   ◇

The worst thing I had to do after you died, Peg, was empty out your apartment. First your father and I packed everything we wanted to keep. I had to restrain your father or he'd have kept everything. Then we gave your bedroom furniture and stereo and lamps to the Lerneys for various of their children, and your waterbed and table and kitchen supplies to John for his apartment after graduation.

John did graduate that year—three months late. He took charge of the final moving day. We hadn't known that it took twenty-four hours to drain a waterbed, and we had to have everything out of the apartment that day, so a couple of friends John rounded up to help stood at the top of the bed and inched that undulating ton of water up and over so that instead of trickling out, the water gushed out of the spout at the foot of the bed, cascaded down a cookie sheet John and Angie manned, and into a cooler. Everyone ended up in their bare feet, shrieking. You'd have loved it.

When we filed out of your apartment, I looked back and saw that the last person had left the door open. So I went back and had a minute to say good-bye. Only . . . your apartment was bare . . . empty of you, Peggie . . . not your apartment anymore.

I went back to Bunting in the fall after your death, parked behind your apartment where I always parked. Walked down the steps to your door. . . . Didn't knock.

I've been deep-cleaning our house. Every time I get rid of something of yours, like the Mr. Spock poster in your bedroom—now the guest room—I cry, but then I tell myself, "Peggie doesn't care about her things anymore."

Remember the toilet brush in the cat holder I bought when Joey was in the hospital for the next-to-last time? And he asked, "Is it a regular cat or a cartoon cat?" And I didn't know, and when he came home for those few days before his last hospitalization, he hurried to the bathroom to see which it was—such a typical Joey concern. I've kept that cat in the downstairs bath all these years, when I don't even use a brush in the bathroom anymore. Well, I just threw out the regular cat. Twelve years after the fact I tell myself, "Joey's not coming back."

We're crazy, Peg, we earthbound humans.

◊   ◊   ◊

Sandy became even sweeter as Peg became sicker and, if possible, more efficient. And Mary, if we needed to know something no one else knew, "Ask Mary what, Mother," Peg said. "Ask Mary where."

There's lots of talk these days about people wanting to go home from the hospital to die, but neither Joey nor Peggie mentioned going home, perhaps because the fourth floor of Rainbow Babies and Children's was a second home to them.

"Dr. Rathburn says he's starting me on MucoMist, Mother—today. But I won't take it unless Mary's sitting beside me the whole time." And Mary, busy mother to the fourth floor, sat beside her the whole time.

Most of the nurses did more than they were obligated to do. Like Georgie who, when she got a speck of betadine on Peg's butterfly sheet, took the sheet home and washed it. Georgie who came in a-flutter one morning because she'd won first prize the night before in a lip-sync contest, Peg as a-flutter for her as for the sister she had never had.

I went around that day humming Georgie's winning number, "Boogie Woogie Bugle Boy From Company B."

"How do you know a song like that, Mother?" Peg asked, amazed as children are always amazed that their parents were young once and boogied, though I had not boogied.

Then there was Eric. For years Peg had been saying, "You have to meet Eric, Mother. I mean, Eric is so . . . well, I can't explain Eric. Why can't you ever be here when Eric's on?"

And, indeed, when I finally met him, Eric exuded a peace you could not explain. Usually he worked second shift, walking down the hall and into our room when our nerves were twitching, soothing us with his slow, steady pace. Eric was one of the God-people on the floor.

Sometimes when the pulmonary therapists couldn't cover all the C.F. patients during the day, the nurses did the patients' last therapies at night. Because Eric never rushed, he didn't get around to therapy till ten or eleven o'clock.

"So, Peg, how'd it go today?" he'd ask, and they'd talk about things of the spirit while he pounded and vibrated Peg's body—her mind as well as her lungs clearer when he left. She loved Eric as the brother she had had and lost.

Angie said a lot of the nurses on the floor were God-people. "Pray for Josh," or "Pray for Angela," they'd ask each other.

Of course there was Trude, a new nurse on the floor—sullen.

"Every family has a Cousin Trude, Peg."

"Yeah," Peg laughed. "And she makes everybody else look even better. Ya know, they still make me get on the scale every morning, but at least they bring it to me instead of dragging me to it. Isn't it wonderful that I haven't gone under ninety pounds, Mother? And I don't look skinny, do I? It'll be okay as long as I don't go under ninety."

Until Peg had gained weight in the past couple years due to improved digestive enzymes, what a *weight* her skinniness had been to her, especially her skinny arms. "No, honey, you don't look skinny, not even your arms." And the strange truth was, she didn't.

I couldn't bear for her to watch herself go under ninety, so I asked Dr. Rathburn not to make her get weighed every day. "Just getting out of bed and on the scale is an ordeal for her." But the doctor said they had to watch for water retention.

Andy and Lou Lerney kept visiting, talking about the tenting vacation Peg would be taking with them again in August. Or Andy came by himself when his work brought him to Cleveland and talked computers with Peg, Peg planning to buy a computer when she got back to her apartment. "I think a Tandy might be best for your purposes, Peggie."

"Andy and Lou sure know how to make a visit Mother. I mean, they just talk, and if I don't feel like answering, they understand and keep talking."

And Brad, Marilyn-from-Washington's brother, came and sat beside Peg while he did his homework, and Peg declared that Brad sure knew how to make a visit too. Talking or not talking wasn't the thing. Companionship was the thing—being one of a pair. "Oh, Mother, isn't it wonderful for Brad to come?"

I learned from Peg's nurses, families, and friends—asking for less and less response from her, leaping to save her the slightest effort.

And I tried not to be jealous of these people whose being there obviously meant more to her than my being there meant. But forget it. Just forget it. She was sick unto death. Forget that noble talk about children finding their own most-cherished people. I was as old as a mother about to outlive both her children—too old for reason. Peg couldn't get a sentence out without gasping for breath, and I was too weary to want anything but for her to love me as much as I loved her.

Jillian from up the hall was better now and stopped in on her way home to say good-bye with hands and face— deaf Jillian. But she hadn't seen Peg for a few days, and her hands flew to her face in shock at what she saw, covered her face so she could not see.

The next day Jillian's boyfriend came back to the hospital in the rain, overly long raincoat flapping, with daffodils in a wine bottle from Jillian because she felt bad about how she had acted.

"I'm sorry Jillian feels bad about that—Mother. It was only—natural. But wasn't it nice for Clay to come over here—when he's been coming every day for so long? Aren't the flowers—bright and cheery?"

We talked when we could. I valued every word.

"Guess what happened this morning, Peg, when I was waiting to get in the Parents Lounge?"

Grin.

"Well, there was this gurney standing conveniently outside the door, so I sat on the end of it."

Bigger grin.

"Did you hear the crash? Good thing I'm so well-padded."

"Ha ha." Teeth clenched. Body stiff.

And then, on the fourth day of Peg's five-day fast-fall, Pastor Arthur came from Bunting to see her, and Peg's cup ranneth over, and words rushed out of her about the glory-quotation and how she was trying to live it out, rushed to the very most wonderful person who had given her the quotation. "Do you remember, Pastor Arthur, how you pounded the pulpit and cried?"

Pastor Arthur did not remember pounding and crying. Pastor Arthur did not remember the quotation.

"Oh, Mother—he came all the way over from Bunting. And I don't even officially belong to his church. Didn't I tell you how wonderful he was? Aren't you thrilled to be meeting all these wonderful people I've been telling you about for so long?"

At the end of his visit, Pastor Arthur asked, "What's the best thing that's happened since you've been in the hospital, Peg?" Not the worst thing, but the best.

Peg thought for a minute, "My mother and I have gotten—closer," she said and glanced at me for confirmation.

And I nodded, as nonchalantly as she had spoken, but, oh, my heart somersaulted within.

14

*A*nd on the last day of Peg's fast-fall . . . well, I couldn't have dreamed of what happened on the last day of Peg's fast-fall.

First, just when I was sure she'd never wash her hair again, she insisted on washing not only her hair but on clambering into that high tub and washing her whole self. It took her the rest of the morning, collapsed in bed, before she could move again.

Then nothing could stop her from getting dressed, shoes and all. She didn't ask Mandy what she should wear. She knew what she would wear: navy cords, navy T-shirt with the "23" on the front, and navy Sub-West jacket. "I know I'm a college graduate now, Mother, but my high school jacket is still my favorite jacket." The only school jacket she had owned.

She'd found the T-shirt shortly before her twenty-third birthday but refused to wear it until she was twenty-three, at a birthday party Angie threw for her.

After dressing, it took her another hour, collapsed in bed, before she could move again. I should have known something was up with her spread out there in jacket and shoes, but I was still recuperating from the tub room and the dressing.

Then she asked me to call Inhalation Therapy for a new tank of oxygen.

"But the tank on your wheelchair is half full, Peggie."

"I know, but I want a full tank."

Then, when a full oxygen tank was tied to her wheelchair, "I want you to take me to Ronald MacDonald House, Mother."

What a schemer, getting where she wanted to go step by manipulating step.

"Well, honey, I don't know, do you think you're up—?"

"Now, Mother, do you know how many times you've said, 'Are you up to this?' 'Are you sure you should do that?' Remember when I was in the hospital with my first central line and I was due to be bridesmaid at Deborah's wedding in New York? You kept asking me if I was up to that trip too, and what would I do about the central line sticking out of my arm?

"Remember how we found the scarf that matched my gown exactly and wrapped it around my shoulders so the central line didn't show? I went to the wedding, and I had the time of my life, Mother. I mean, I know a clot formed in my central line. I know there was a risk, but some things are worth the risk.

"You may recall, Mother, that you didn't even want me to go to my college graduation."

No, I did not recall. Recalled, in fact, hoping against hope that she'd be able to leave the hospital for her graduation, but I didn't correct her, sensing that she needed to muster major defiance to propel her on today's excursion.

"And me working as hard as I did to get through college with all those long hospitalizations I kept having, and with my pizza party after graduation and all. How could you have wanted me to miss the best day of my life? You're always tryin' to keep me from doin' stuff."

Then when the grand moment for our departure for Ronald MacDonald House arrived, she announced, "Now, Mother, I may have to be in a wheelchair, but I do not have to look more like an invalid than necessary. So let's take my tissues and mucus cup and all and put them in my knapsack."

And off we went, Peg waving show-offishly to patients

and nurses as we lurched down the hall, fluorescent blue knapsack flapping against the oxygen tank on the back of her wheelchair.

"I want to show you the route Marilyn and I took when we did this, Mother," she said, guiding me through two hospitals attached to Rainbow Babies and Children's, out a side door, through an empty lot, and into the back door of Ronald MacDonald House. "I mean, did we find the shortcuts or what?"

And then she introduced me to the manager and showed me the laundry room and the parlors and the kitchen, "Where I fixed Marilyn chicken cacciatore in the microwave, Mother. Just look at how Stouffers stocks the freezer."

And then I had to fix her chicken cacciatore, and though she looked at it for a while, I ended up eating it, though I was almost as unable to eat as she, having had lunch just before we left the hospital, and being weak and covered with worry-sweat alone with Peggie so far from the hospital in her wheelchair with the oxygen tank on the back.

I knew why they watched Peg for water retention, because they were afraid she'd go into pulmonary heart failure. I knew this because Joey had gone into pulmonary heart failure from water retention. I was sick to my stuffed stomach wanting to get Peg back to the hospital, and how she would pay for this outing when we did get back and her need to relive a happy time and her adrenalin gave out.

But for now Peg wanted only to sit at the kitchen table and talk as she had sat there and talked with Marilyn. "Ya know how many times I've been a bridesmaid, Mother? Six, I think, and later this month for Shelley is seven."

Not *would be* seven, not *will be* seven. *Is* seven.

"Ya know what they say: Always a bridesmaid, never a maid of honor. Have you noticed that no matter how much my friends like me, they always have somebody they like better? Let's take the long way home, Mother. There's a path through a park I want to show you."

It was a spring day. It was a warm, sweet, tender spring day. It was the good earth's "good morning" of the year, the *baby* park Peg directed us to stretching its gold-green arms up-up to the sun, chubby daffodil feet scampering every-where.

"Slow down, Mother. Meander," Peg urged, lifting her face to lilac-scented breezes, then lowering her face to sniff the dirt, to salute the daffodils.

When she was in high school, Peg saluted the first day of spring by delivering to each of her friends a florist-bought daffodil, each flower wrapped with a fern in the thin green paper florists use.

Actually, the first day of spring had a way of coinciding with spring vacation, and since Peg synchronized her hospitalizations with school vacations, usually I ended up delivering the daffodils from one end of Parma Heights to the other.

"Did you remember to say 'Happy First Day of Spring' as you gave each person their daffodil, Mother? Did you go back to places where no one was home? Come on, come on, did the kids' faces light up or what?"

Even when we left the park, dogwood and apple trees bloomed in squares of earth set into concrete walks, *children* trees raising their boy-girl voices in praise of new life.

A hot dog vendor held forth on the sidewalk near Rainbow. "Come on, Mother, buy a hot dog," Peg begged. "I mean, it's a lot different buying a hot dog from a sidewalk vendor than taking one out of the refrigerator at home."

I choked down every bite, but, oh, the eagerness on Peg's face as she *ate* the hot dog with me, on the sidewalk, on a spring day, double the mustard.

How synthetic the air felt as I pushed Peg back into the hospital. I looked down on her as we waited for the elevator, and she looked gray now, nursing-home old, her clothes hanging on her body, held into the wheelchair only by the straps of her will to get back to her room erect.

As I looked down at her, I thought, surprised at my thought, not knowing where it had come from, *The glory of God is a human being fully alive.*

"Do you remember, Mother," she asked, back in her bed with only shoes and jacket removed, "when Joey and I were little and you drove us to the hospital for checkups and got us to count the interesting things we saw on the way? Remember the time there was white snow everywhere, and this little kid was walking home from school, and all in a twinkle she dropped her school bag—threw herself down— on her back in the snow—moved her arms up and down— and just as quickly leaped up—looked down on the angel— she had made—and walked on.

"Do you remember—Mother—the angel in the snow?" she asked, gasping for breath after every few words. The last words she spoke that day.

"Yes, Peggie, I remember."

"Excuse me, Peggie. I'm going to the Parents Lounge and get the mustard out of these pants."

"Keep an eye on her, will you, Angie?" I called as I sped down the hall. "She's dangerously tired."

I scrubbed away at the mustard so I would have told the truth about why I came to the Parents Lounge, but soon I fell onto the couch and did once more what we parents did best in our lounge. I wept.

Yes, I would always remember the angel in the snow.

I would always remember, too, a more recent drive with Peg when a song on the radio had captured her imagination with lyrics about fun and seasons in the sun. Peg hastily scribbled down what words she could.

"What happened, Mother? Did somebody die? Did they break up?"

After that, whenever the song drifted our way, Peg nudged me and said, "Have you figured it out yet, Mother?"

◊   ◊   ◊

When I was doing my deep cleaning the other day, Peg, sorting out the storage cabinet of the stereo, I came upon another song you scribbled out and made me listen to over and over.

There's a ship lies rigged and ready in the harbour
Tomorrow for old England she sails
Far away from your land of endless sunshine
To my land full of rainy skies and gales

137

And I shall be on board that ship tomorrow
Though my heart is full of tears at this farewell
For you are beautiful,
And I have loved you dearly,
More dearly than the spoken word can tell.

I heard there's a wicked war ablazing
And the taste of war I know so very well
Even now I see the foreign flag araising
Their guns on fire as we sailed into hell.
I have no fear of death,
It brings no sorrow
But how bitter will be this last farewell
For you are beautiful,
And I have loved you dearly,
More dearly than the spoken word can tell.
For you are beautiful,
And I have loved you dearly,
More dearly than the spoken word can tell.

I went to a Roger Whittaker concert last year, Peg. Can you believe I heard Roger Whittaker sing "The Last Farewell" in person!

Oh, Peggie, I'm so glad you had that last day in the spring sun. But how I lifted up my head and wept loud in the Parents Lounge because you would never touch or smell another spring, because you and I would never go anywhere together again, spring or winter, summer, fall.

John has a new job—Advertising Manager for Rainbow Babies and Children's Hospital. He tried to imagine what you'd say to that. "Boy!" . . . "Wow!" . . . "I'm impressed!"

I write with a computer now, Peg. You were wrong all those times you told me I'd been born too late for the computer age. And I'm going back to school to study to be a counselor. I'll always write, but I want to do something with people, too, something that will enable me to use for their good the things I've learned from my experiences with you and Joey. I want to do for other people what Ben has done for me.

I'm fifty-seven. "So!" Ben says. "Good for you. You've

set your course for the next thirty years!"

I don't know about that, but your old mother is going to have one last season of her own in the sun.

◇   ◇   ◇

Dr. Howard Trentowsky, the president of Bunting College, came to see Peggie that night. Had she not already been speechless, disbelief and pride would have rendered her so. First her beloved Pastor Arthur and now her beloved college president—coming to see *her*.

Dr. Trentowsky asked Peggie if there was anything she wanted him to pray for, and, at the end of the last day of her fast-fall, her last day of spring, too weak to whisper, she motioned me down to read her lips.

"To pray—that I'll—make the glory. I'm—still not sure—I'm doin' it."

15

*P*eg stopped falling then. There was no place further down that she could fall.

For five days she ate nothing.

"How long can a person live without eating, Dr. Rathburn? Why don't you feed her intravenously?"

"There's a risk of water retention with intravenous feeding, Mrs. Woodson. I can't take the risk with the strain Peg's labored breathing is putting on her heart."

And then Dr. Rathburn left for Kansas City for the annual National Cystic Fibrosis Conference. Every doctor in the country connected with cystic fibrosis went. Dr. Rathburn went earlier than the other doctors in our hospital because he was giving a paper.

"I'll call you every night," he promised Peggie, and to me in the hall he said, "I don't know how this is going to turn out."

The director of the C.F. Center at Rainbow took over for Dr. Rathburn for the next two days, paging me both mornings from the nurses' station to discuss Peg's case.

"What's goin' on?" Peg demanded.

"Your potassium level is low, Peg. The doctor's going to start you on a potassium drip."

"He already told me that. Why tell you?"

"Strange goings on," I said, and she couldn't help grinning.

I don't know what the director said to Peg when *he* left for Kansas City, but to me he had said, "It doesn't look good."

It doesn't look good. . . . I don't know how this is going to turn out. . . . I think we've got one.

Dr. Grollier, a fellow in the C.F. Center, and Dr. Abinsky, our house doctor, took over next. We liked them, but we felt as though we had been left to fight our archenemy in the last minutes of a losing game with a substitute team.

"Will Peggie die today?" I asked.

"Probably not today."

"Tomorrow?"

"Probably not tomorrow."

"Well, when, then? Keep your *probablys* and tell me when."

"She probably has a few days, Mrs. Woodson."

"Have you ever known a patient as sick as Peggie to recover, Dr. Abinsky?"

"No."

"Isn't there anything you can do for her, Dr. Grollier?"

"No. We're not in a position to change her treatment till Dr. Rathburn gets back."

Peg's game was up. No chance of turning the tide with our present strategy, and no chance of changing our strategy till the coach came home. *Swear. Swear.*

And all the while, Peg, who could not get weaker, did.

And didn't eat. Didn't eat. And one of the doctors—who knows which one—said, "If you have to choose between breathing and eating, you choose breathing. The need for air is the most elemental of human needs."

I helped Peg sit up when she wanted to use her potty chair, but she couldn't summon the energy to get from bed to chair. I couldn't leave her to get a nurse lest she topple over, so Peg sat there swaying back and forth—I not touching her but ready to grab her—till a nurse walked in. Sometimes we waited half an hour for a nurse to lift Peg from bed to potty chair and back to bed.

I should have been able to do that. Why were some things so hard for me to do? Why didn't I ring for a nurse?

At times I was as nonfunctional as Peg.

But I did not leave her. I dressed and undressed in her bathroom. I brushed my teeth in the sink in the far corner of her room. I ate the food that came up on her tray.

"As long as we're payin' for it—Mother—I think it's honest for you to eat it. Here—you fill in the menu. You might as well—eat what you like."

I left her only when Joe or John were with her, and then only to run errands for her, and even then I took *Abandonment to Divine Providence* with me. Sometimes I slept with it in bed with me at night.

We kept the curtain drawn between Joanne's bed and Peg's all the time now, but when the phone rang, Joanne's hand reached behind the curtain to answer it—my social secretary to the end. She went home sometime in the five days of Peg's bottom-out period. Every loss of anyone rubbed more raw that scraped-bare spot in my heart that waited for the loss of Peggie.

The room was not the same without Joanne, though it did feel cozy with just the Canfields and us there.

One night—the coziness was greater at night—Peg asked me to wash her feet, and I washed them and rubbed lotion on them. I'd never washed anybody's feet before, not *just* their feet. I wondered if Christ washing the disciples' feet before His death made Him feel as close to them as I felt to Peg.

I told her then what I'd been waiting for the perfect moment to tell her—that I was sorry I hadn't been a better mother.

"But you've been—a good mother," she said.

"Yes, Peggie, but so many times with my actions I've said, 'Get out of my way, Peggie. Let me do my important things.' "

And she said, "Yes—that's true."

"You know, Peg, in a way I've never felt more satisfied than I've felt living in with you during this hospitalization. There's something healing about taking care of a sick offspring."

"That's weird," Peg said, and then, "ya know, I've been

wanting to tell you—that you were a good mother, but I didn't want it to sound—like a deathbed scene. But then we might as well have our deathbed scene now—so that if the time comes—and we can't have it, we will already have had it."

It was vintage Peggie. I would never find another like her, search the world as I would for as long as I was in it.

Peg asked me to hold her hand a lot during this period, even in the daytime . . . to sit close . . . rub her legs. Strange, strange goings on.

The night of the foot-washing and the deathbed scene, as I crawled into my cot, her voice followed me. "I love you, Mother. Try not to feel too bad."

I still propped at least ten pillows around her at night, but now instead of leaning back against them, she leaned over them, over one or another of the side rails on her bed. That night she leaned over the side rail facing my cot, that night she said, "I love you, Mother."

◊　　◊　　◊

Talking about strange goings on, Peg, I can't remember holding your hand, touching you in any way except in taking care of you. But it's in the record of your hospitalization I taped after you died; I didn't make it up. But you'd been no-touch for so long. . . . I don't know, maybe some glories are too bright to look back on.

I don't remember you saying I love you either. I remember everything else I recorded your saying, but not that.

I took care of you in the hospital, Peg, but you took care of me too.

◊　　◊　　◊

On the afternoon before Dr. Rathburn came back, Peg said to Cheryl, "This room is too crowded—with unnecessary stuff since Joanne went home."

"You want me to move something out, Peg?"

"How about Joanne's bed?"

"Okay," said Cheryl, and she wheeled Joanne's bed out of the room. "Anything else, Peg?"

"Joanne's bed tray."

"Okay," said Cheryl, and Joanne's bed tray followed her bed.

"Is that it, Peg?"

"How about moving my mother's cot—to where Joanne's bed was?"

And it was done. *Glory be*, as my grandmother would have said.

No longer did I sleep on chug-a-lugging Public Square, but in my own private corner of the room, with my own curtain to pull to make it more private still, with my own bedside cabinet to put my private things in, and my own bed lamp with which to lighten or darken my very own private place.

After that, whenever Angie gave report, she said, "And in room 420, bed 1, we have Meg Woodson."

I waited every day for a real patient to check in and take away my space, but for the fourteen days left to us, no one took away from me the gift of love my daughter gave me.

16

*H*ow nearly dead can a daughter be and still be purely Peggie?

Not once during those five nearly dead days did Peg relinquish control of her situation.

I brought toothpaste and brush to her now, along with a cup of water for her to rinse with and another cup for her to spit the rinse water into. So maybe she couldn't walk to the sink or get there in her wheelchair, but what she could do for herself she would do, and no one had better try to do it for her.

And no one had better try to keep her from looking on the bright side of things.

"My hair itched a lot—the first couple—days I didn't wash it, but it feels better now. Some of the kids told me it would be like that. Isn't it neat—that my hair doesn't itch so much now?"

And better that no one suggest that the tissues I bought her at the drugstore didn't smell. If she could smell them, they smelled. If she went into a coughing fit every time she got one near her nose, they smelled. Hospital tissues didn't smell but were rough.

On every one of the five days Dr. Rathburn was gone, the five days that coincided with Peg's all-the-way-down days, she commissioned me to make one more trip to the drugstore to buy "a box of *unscented* tissues, Mother—tissues with *no scent at all*."

I opened every box of tissues and sniffed before I bought them, two or three boxes a trip, surreptitiously lest I be put out of the store as a sniff freak.

But, "It sure is strange—you can't smell that, Mother?" Peg said as rejected boxes of yellow and pink and green and blue and lilac tissues packed her closet shelf.

"You can't smell that either, Angie? Honestly! John, you can't smell *that*?"

It took me forty-five minutes to get to the drugstore, do my *snorting*, and get back to Peggie. I only went when Joe or John was with her, but terror that Peg would die while I was gone and I would not be there to God-speed her on her way engulfed me.

And worse than the terror was the joy that engulfed me. To walk in an unsealed world—I wanted to skip—with *vertical* people on their way to the drugstore to buy Coke and Dristan and all-natural wheat bread. What if Peg called "Mother" just before she died or held out her hand to me and I was having a fine old time away from that tomb of a hospital?

Once I stopped at the reception desk on my way back from the drugstore to pick up a reduced-cost parking ticket for John. They only issued one ticket a family a day, and that day the receptionist said, "Oh, I can't give you a ticket. Your daughter's husband already picked one up."

She meant John, of course, who gave a big belly laugh when I told him and Peg about it, and Peg hooted too, before she could stop herself. For days she told every person who came into the room how the woman at the desk had said she'd given a parking ticket *"to my husband."* I suspect there was wistfulness in the telling, but I do not think Peg suspected it. One of my griefs for her was that her desire to be *chosen that way* was so great that she could only live with it by burying it.

Instead of holding her arms stiff to her sides to keep from coughing when she laughed now, she folded her arms over her chest. With her face ashen and her arms crossed, she looked like a corpse laughing, and no matter what defensive position her arms took, her cough won vicious victories.

Don't let yourself laugh, Peggie, a part of me pleaded. And most of the time she lay like an animal who'd thumped at murderous speed down a killer-cliff, smashed into all-but-unconsciousness. But then she would drift back into Peggiehood, and best I not plead out loud that she not laugh, or hint that she was wrong when she was right, or act like things were worse than they were. I mean, on top of everything else, suppose her head did itch?

Joe phoned between his daily visits to the hospital now.

"I wonder if Father—is such a good minister to everyone—or just to me," Peg said after one of his phone calls. "I mean, he asked me if I was scared—and I was—but I didn't know it till he asked me. How did he know? I don't know what I was afraid of—but Father read me one of his fear-not verses—from the Bible—and then I wasn't afraid anymore."

Peg's God-hunger did not abate. I thanked God for that above all else.

"I miss church," she said on Sunday morning. So I rented the color TV over her bed, and we watched Robert Schuller's "Hour of Power" together.

"I used to make fun of his little slogans a little—Mother—but lots of times since I've been layin' here—I've been thinking—*Inch by inch, everything's a cinch.* Do you know how long it's been—since I heard a hymn? Wasn't it wonderful?"

And at least once a day she asked me to read from "my book," and I picked quotations about living for the present moment.

"The disclosure that each moment brings is of such great value because it is meant for us personally."

"Yeah, yeah."

"The present moment is an ever-flowing source of holiness."

"Yeah."

◇　　◇　　◇

149

Friends kept calling and visiting, and we didn't cut them off because as tired as we were, and as more tired as they made us, we needed them.

There were only two people Peg did not need: Aunt Trude and the Reverend Olivet.

Peg's antibiotics gave her urine a pungent odor, and one morning she told me she'd lain awake for three hours, by the clock on her bed tray, waiting for Trude to empty her potty chair. "What a bother she makes me feel, Mother."

"No one as sick as Peggie ought to have to contend with Trude," I complained to Mary.

But Mary said she couldn't let one patient choose her nurse without letting all patients choose their nurses.

"But someone as sick as Peggie?"

At which Mary took me out into the hall and pointed to a room across the hall, a room up the hall, a room down the hall, all of which contained patients as sick as Peggie.

"Well, then, Trude shouldn't be on the floor at all," I raged.

"How poorly Trude must have been cared for in her lifetime to care so poorly for others now," I said to Peg one night as I fumbled out of bed to empty her potty chair myself.

"Yeah."

"I keep wishing I could care for her now."

"Me too."

"But I don't."

"Me neither."

We giggled some over Trude, but for Peg the Reverend Olivet was serious business.

One of the older ministers in our denomination, he came to see Peg often and he stayed long—a rotund little man rolling into the room smiling from cheek to chubby cheek and giving a yay-yay-isn't-the-Christian-life-wonderful sermonette. Before he left, he made us all stand in a circle around Peg and hold hands while he prayed. Peg hated it.

"When Reverend Woodson prays, it's like a continuation of his conversation," John said. "But when Reverend Olivet prays, it's a production."

John took the spontaneous praying that went on in the room in stride. We called him our token Catholic, and he said, "Oh, it's a rotten job, but somebody has to do it."

"Okay—Mother," Peg gasped after one of Reverend Olivet's visits, "get a paper towel. I want you to make a list of the characteristics—of a good ministerial call. Then when he comes next time—I'll read it to him."

"Oh, honey, he means well."

"Yeah, but he's not doin' well—and if he hasn't learned by his age, he never will—unless somebody tells him. Okay, put down: 1. Be real. Do not act like everything is wonderful if it's not. 2. Develop a sense of when patient is tired, and leave. 3. Don't come as a duty—only if you care. 4.—"

"If you tell Reverend Olivet what he's doing wrong, Peg, he'll feel less good about himself than he already does and do even more things wrong. If you want to help him, pick out one thing he does right and tell him you appreciate that."

"Yeah—but what one thing?"

Still, Peg did not on this occasion persist with her list; nor on future occasions did she instruct the Reverend Mr. Browning Olivet on the proprieties of hospital visitation.

And then at the end of what seemed Peg's coming-to-an-end days, even she could not have outlined a more perfect hospital visit than the one she received—for Edith Schaeffer came to call.

The well-known writer and speaker, wife of Francis Schaeffer, had given the graduation address at Bunting College, and Dr. Trentowsky brought her by on their way to the Cleveland airport.

She blew into the room holding out a branch of dogwood that looked like she'd just clipped it from a tree, but in a vase so you knew she'd planned to bring it. And this stranger, this celebrity, hugged and kissed me and hugged and kissed Peggie, and seemed not a stranger at all.

"I'm going to put on my academic regalia, Peggie," she said, hanging the colored strips of cloth around her neck, wanting Peggie to have a sense of having been there when she delivered her address, which she delivered again in condensed form to a bedazzled audience of one.

Except that Joe and John and I hung on every word too, about the despair of today's rock music, and Carl Sagan asking, "Is anybody out there?" And about a young man she had known who was dying and how eagerly he had looked forward not just to going to heaven, but to *being with the Lord*.

Somebody was out there, and, oh, the excitement and wonder of being with Him.

Dr. Trentowsky grew worried that Edith would miss her plane, but she cared about nothing but the young woman, who, in her honor, was sitting plumb-straight-up in her bed.

"There's a Peggie Woodson inside Peggie Woodson's body right now that's longing to get out and can't, isn't there, Peggie?" she asked.

By this time Dr. Trentowsky was making frantic movements to get Edith going, and she hugged and kissed Peggie good-bye, and I ran with her to the elevator, she taking off her regalia as she ran, telling me as we stood by the elevator that she had come from seeing students honored for academic achievements and achievements in sports, but Peggie. . . . Dr. Trentowsky had told her about Peg's glory-making, and, oh, what recognition Peggie would receive on her *graduation day*.

The elevator came, but Edith kept hugging me and would not get on, and the elevator went and came again and Dr. Trentowsky pulled her on, and she threw kisses till the door closed.

Peg was still sitting straight up when I got back to her, Joe and John still standing, stunned into immobility.

"There was an aura of holiness—about her, Mother," Peg breathed.

It was so. I had not known that holiness could sweep in and out of your life like a spattering of sun-filled rain leaving you feeling cleansed, alive.

"How did she know that, Father—about there being a Peggie Woodson inside me that was longing to get out—and couldn't?"

Later Edith Schaeffer sent Peg a copy of one of her

books. The autograph went on for pages.

◇   ◇   ◇

During the first half of Peg's hospitalization, it was more my friends than hers that came to call, Peg having conditioned her friends not to think of her hospitalizations as cause for concern or visitation. But now they came.

"It's as though somebody pushed a button—isn't it, Mother? Did you notice how everybody started comin'—right after Dr. Trentowsky prayed—I'd make the glory? Some coincidence, eh, Mother?"

When Lester, one of Peg's old gang from ninth-grade Advanced English and the first of those Peg thought of as *the sent ones*, arrived, she asked, "Will you pull the curtain—around my bed please? I'd like to talk to Les—in private."

John and I sat on my cot—not to eavesdrop, we just dropped there—but we did hear Peg tell Les that if she died . . . she didn't think she would, but just in case . . . she wanted him to know that she wasn't afraid. There was more, something about a cameo and a meadow, but she talked in such depleted tones that her words didn't carry.

Les zigzagged out from behind the curtain and down the hall as though he were on his way to his death, but Peg beamed. She had done what she could to make her death, should it happen, easier for Les.

John was still on my cot with his head in his hands when I opened Peg's curtain, and she must have seen from the way I too drooped that we had heard.

"Before you say anything—Mother," she sputtered, "if you had a friend who died, wouldn't the thing that helped you most—be knowin' that she hadn't been afraid? I realize Dr. Rathburn said—I should save my energy for therapy—but some things are more important. Honestly, Mother."

From then on when her friends came, she said, "Would you step into the hall, Mother, please?" And she would have her private conferences, buoyed up when her friends left, briefly buoyed up, and then foundering in heavy seas.

On the last of Peg's bottom-of-the-cliff days, Joe and I were in the hall when a delegation of her friends from Bunting poured out of the elevator and flooded the hall, seven or eight of them spread out side to side and front to back carrying huge handmade get-well cards and crazily wrapped packages and balloons flying high.

"We've got to stop them," Joe said. "She can't handle that many people."

"She has to," I said, but we both kept watch from the corner of the room for as long as they were there.

I'd lost touch with high spirits and high jinks, with young people with futures, laughing in a group, catching Peg up on their lives.

Then, when they wound down, Peggie talked to them. I'd forgotten how hushed a group of vital young people could become, how they could lean forward en masse absorbing things of the spirit, how they could cry. And, when they left, how they could care.

I walked them to the elevator, a more controlled flood now, moving together down the right side of the hall.

"Bunting wouldn't have been Bunting without Peggie."

"Yeah, she was always so happy she made everybody around her happy."

"Remember the time she couldn't climb the stairs to *The Trumpeter* office and I carried her up piggyback? You could hear her screaming all over campus."

"Yeah, she was always always screaming, especially when I nagged her to cover her mouth with her scarf in the winter."

Laughter.

"She talked so fast, I couldn't always keep up with her."

"Yeah, and she loved bright colors."

"Remember how excited she got over the scale model of the solar system she fastened to the ceiling of her room?"

Laughter.

"She listened to me complain and cared about my problems, but then she always cheered me up."

Pause.

"She was always a good, sweet person to me."

And then they coursed into the elevator, minus balloons and fruit baskets, and were gone.

Oh, God, Peggie has so much to give. Why can't she have a future too? I scuffed my way slowly back down the hall. *What does the English Award she got in high school mean now, God? The Communications Award in college? Her achievements meant so much to her. She worked so hard to excel. What does any of it mean now?*

I sat down close to Peggie then to see how she was, bent down close to listen to her gasp out her words.

"I think—I'm finally—making the glory—*Ma*," she gasped. "And—as though—that wasn't enough," she added, grinning at me in her old impish way, "with all—those people—here to see me—I actually felt—*popular*."

17

*T*hat night as Peg lay gasping out nothing but shallow breath upon shallow, rasping breath, her eyes open, but, as far as we could tell, unseeing, Joe and John and I gathered in the waiting room down the hall for a conference.

"We can't let Peggie die without telling her she's dying," Joe said.

"Peg's always gotten furious if anyone hid anything about her condition from her," John said.

But I said, "No."

Dr. Rathburn said that when patients wanted to know if they were dying, they asked. And Peggie always said that C.F. kids knew without asking—that no matter how many times everyone else thought they were dying, if they weren't, they knew they weren't, and if they were, they knew that too.

"She knows that the odds are against her," I said. "She verbalizes that knowledge every time a friend comes near her. But what if she has a chance of living and we take away her hope?" *Dear God, what if telling her she's dying makes it so?*

◇   ◇   ◇

And so, Peg, I, who was the first to know you could not be saved, was the last to give up on saving you. We were cast overboard, you and I, in a drowning sea, and I knew no help would come, but could I let you slip under the waves while I had any grip left? I never gave up on you, Peggie. I was your mother.

◇   ◇   ◇

John looked so stricken leaning against the wall of the waiting room that I decided the time had come to deliver Peg's *John-is-my-most-cherished-person* message.

But then I didn't know whether I'd consoled John or demolished him, because his face turned splotchy red and he choked on his words. "I don't want to intrude . . . into your family life, Reverend and Mrs. Woodson, but if it's so . . . that you can let me know, I'd like to be with Peggie . . . when she dies. I'd like to see this through . . . to the end."

"Of course, John. We'll need you here," I said, my voice shaking too. How I wished I could make his grief less, but it was a part of his love for Peggie, of who he was.

"You know, people," I said as we walked back to Peggie's room, "when Marilyn-from-Washington's brother was here, he told me that what worried Peg most about dying was the pain she'd cause those she left behind. Maybe not talking to us about her death is her way of trying to save us pain. Let's play this Peg's way."

But the drama unfolding was a tragedy, no matter how we played it, and when Joe and John left and I no longer had an audience to play to, my stage fright intensified—till at eleven or twelve that night Dr. Abinsky found me roving the halls with what must have been delirium in my eyes because she led me down to the consultation room to talk.

"Is something wrong, Mrs. Woodson?"

Is something wrong? What could be more wrong?

"Yes, something is wrong. Peggie is dying. Right now. And no one will make a move to stop her till Dr. Rathburn gets back."

"Do you want me to call Dr. Rathburn in Kansas City?"

"Yes, I want you to call Dr. Rathburn in Kansas City."

"Do you want me to call him at this time of night in Kansas City?"

"Yes, I want you to call him at this time of night in Kansas City."

What difference does the time of night make? Don't you hear me? Peggie is dying.

What happened after that is lost to me. I remember nothing from that midnight till the next evening when Dr. Rathburn came back—and Peg sat up and talked to him chipper as could be.

"That's not the way rumor had it in Kansas City," he said to me in the hall.

But even so, and even though he was due to come back that day or the next, I felt satisfaction in having taken control. Goodness knows, he needed the time away. His patients were his life. I didn't fault him for going away, but I was glad he was back.

The next morning when Dr. Rathburn made rounds, Peg was too out of it to know I was in the room, and I heard him say, "These are our options: we can increase one of your meds and run the risk of kidney failure; we can increase the second of your meds and run the risk of liver failure; we can increase the third of your meds and run the risk of deafness. Or we can discontinue all your present medications and try to get some ceftazidime. I'll see what's available.

"Meanwhile, I'm starting you on one of the cortisones to reduce the inflammation in your lungs, and I'm getting an experimental machine down here—a Domicron—that will feed you oxygen and humidity from the atmosphere. It keeps the oxygen moist and at room temperature and won't harden the mucus in your lungs."

Peggie gasped out a tiny "Yeah" without lifting her head from the pillow on her bed tray. "Yeah" for the Domicron, and "Let's go—for the—ceftazidime."

And picking up Peg's phone, Dr. Rathburn said, "I don't care who the Domicron's earmarked for, I want it here for Peggie Woodson now."

Deafness. The word shouted out all other words the doctor spoke. It reminded me of how levelheadedly I'd handled C.F. when the children were little, but lost control when they got the chicken pox. *Not deafness. Not like Jillian. Not on top of everything else.*

159

"That's the way rumor had it when you were in Kansas City," I said to Dr. Rathburn in the hall, sure now I'd been right in not taking away Peggie's hope. Something was being done.

I was even more sure later in the morning when Peggie revived enough to say, "I don't think I'll ever be able—to take care of myself again without help, and I want to go back to my apartment—so call Canterbury Manors, Mother, and rent the empty apartment—across the hall, and maybe Jody or somebody else from college—will move in and I'll pay the rent and they can shop and clean for me."

◊　◊　◊

"I'm calling for one of your tenants—Peggie Woodson," I told Lisa at Canterbury Manors. "I know you run a huge complex so you probably can't place her—"

"Oh, I know Peggie," Lisa said. "She sends cheery notes with her rent, and smile faces. And with her last check she sent a yellow card in celebration of spring. Everybody here knows Peggie."

Peg had celebrated spring this year by sending bright yellow postcards to everyone she knew, proclaiming: *Spring is for dream launching.*

I explained Peg's situation and her desire to rent the apartment across the hall, but Lisa said it had just been rented to someone named Davis, and that in an unprecedented occurrence the agent who rented it had failed to get Davis's address or phone number or first name.

"But," said Lisa, "tell Peggie not to worry. I'll see what I can do."

"Good," said Peg. "Get a paper towel, Mother. I want to make a list of the good things—that have happened since I've been in the hospital." And I listed for her her wonderful room—and the names of her friends who had visited, and how nice Lisa was being—and John. "There's too much to say about John to list it all—so just say *John*. The flowers he gave me—are so nice. He never gave me flowers before."

And in the same strained tones she went on to say that she still worried that there might be things in John's life more important to him than God, and that if God became first in his life through this hospitalization, it would be worth it all.

"And put *Edith Schaeffer* down too, Mother. And save the towel. I'm sure there'll be more good things—to add to the list."

Peg knew how to keep her spirits high: Plan for the future. Think about what's good in the present, and give purpose to what's not good. Could we have taken away Peg's hope had we tried? Still the *Pegginess* of the list unstrung me. Angie found me weaving through the halls this time, and she too, led me to the consultation room.

"What's your best coping device, Mrs. Woodson?"

"Knowing I'll be able to make something good come out of the bad. At least that's always helped till now." How alike Peg's and my instincts were.

"Man, that's a good way to cope," Angie said, glossy brown hair bobbing at me approvingly.

I craved approval.

Then Angie showed me the pictures she'd taken of Peggie at the party she'd given for her on her twenty-third birthday. Pictures of Peggie hamming it up in her navy T-shirt with the 23 on the front. And one picture of Peggie in the red blouse with the white collar we had found on sale at The Gap.

Angie explained that Peg had changed clothes during the picture-taking and said, "Take one of me in this blouse for my mother."

Man, that Angie knew how to help me cope.

◊   ◊   ◊

Is that why I had you buried in that blouse, Peg? Because it meant you thought of me in the midst of all your friends on your last . . . on your last birthday?

◊   ◊   ◊

Still, nothing helped me cope for long that day, especially when Dr. Rathburn said, "I think she has a chance."

"How much of a chance?"

"Ten percent, maybe twenty, thirty. It depends on whether or not I can get the ceftazidime."

For so long I'd heard *no chance* that hearing *some chance* was the last straw. It made no sense. Who wanted to make sense?

I just wanted to get to the Parents Lounge and slam the door, which I did. Banged it shut, hunkered down inside myself on the couch, and shut out hope—shut out no hope. *But please, God, whatever happens, don't let Peg go deaf. And about the ceftazidime, God. We need some.*

I was incoherent when God came to me. Like at mass, only His presence filled every nook and cranny of the room. Oh, no outer light. No vision of our Lord. I didn't need an outer light. I didn't, for those moments, need anything but His peace glowing in every nook and cranny of me.

Everything was all right. How could I feel that way? Yet I melted inside at the peace that came to me. And for as long as I stayed in the Parents Lounge, God stayed with me. I knew He was always with me, but the sense of His nearness had never been so sweet.

In the end, since I had to get back to Peggie, and He did not leave me, I left Him. I will never forget leaving Him. Walking away from the presence of God was the loneliest thing I have ever done.

Though soon I discovered, and it was so till the end of Peg's hospitalization, that I had only to recall His presence in the Parents Lounge to call His presence, in some measure, back to me.

Even when things were at their worst, as they were when I returned to Peg slumped over her bed tray, *not there* as far as I could tell, not there for me. It mattered that she wasn't there. Would I live the rest of my life with a daughter or . . . a blank . . . by my side? Yet when I called God back, He came, and with Him an inner stillness.

Even when things were at their best, as when Dr. Rathburn rushed in early in the afternoon to announce that he'd gotten so much ceftazidime he would give it to Peg in quadruple the amount it had been given to anyone anywhere.

Even when Lisa called from Canterbury Manors late in

the afternoon to say she'd spent the day calling every Davis in the Bunting phone book, and then in phone books in surrounding areas, till she'd located the right Davis and talked her into renting a unit in another building.

"I wonder why they're being so nice to me. Didn't I tell you they were wonderful at Canterbury, Mother?"

I hadn't believed her before. Peggie generally thought people were wonderful, but I believed her now, and again when a bright yellow floral arrangement arrived from "Lisa and Company."

"Find my checkbook, Mother—and send them a deposit and two months rent. It may be a while—before I get back there."

◇　◇　◇

They sent the check back after you died, Peg. I told them they weren't being fair to themselves, that they'd lost rent on that apartment, but they said they'd decide what was fair and returned the whole amount, even the month's rent you paid on your own apartment. I hope you know how nice people were to you after your death, Peggie.

◇　◇　◇

Several of Peg's friends sent her floral arrangements, and we lined them up on the far side of the room because we didn't know if they affected her breathing. What a happy mural they made. A little bouquet of loosely arranged spring flowers from Jody was over against the far wall, too.

Was it a mural of hope? Was that what the Presence meant? That the ceftazidime would come? That the apartment would be available? That Peggie would live?

I had learned during Joey's last hospitalization that God's coming to you did not mean your child would live, only that God would come to you whether or not your child lived. But I should not say *only*. Never *only*.

For at suppertime I was due to pick up homemade strudel from a friend at the entrance to the hospital at 5:30 sharp. I was racing for the elevator when I realized I needed to stop in the restroom. I raced past the elevator to the

Ladies Room, but someone was in there, so I sprinted farther on down the hall to use the bathroom in the Parents Lounge.

I yanked open the door, intent on nothing but the bathroom . . . and He was still there. Without my thinking about Him, without my asking for Him. . . . *Dear God, did You spend all day in the Parents Lounge waiting for me to come back?*

It was *only* the most wonder-filled thing that ever happened to me.

When night settled in on the floor, I told Peg about the Parents Lounge. She was leaning over a pillow on her bed rail, inert, but even when she couldn't talk, she seemed to like me to talk to her.

"Remember the classical music station we picked up on our trip last winter, honey, and the announcer saying he would only play music that spoke of peace, calm, serenity, tranquillity? And we joked about how he must have a thesaurus at hand?

"And then the music spoke such peace to us that when we stopped for lunch at the Holiday Inn in Erie, we didn't get out of the car but sat in a wooded area by a brook absorbing not only the quiet of the music inside the car but of the snow-blanketed trees outside, of the ice-carpeted brook that wound its way through the trees."

I knew she remembered because it was the most perfect time we had had together and we reminisced about it often. "Well, that's what it was like in the Parents Lounge, Peg, only more calm and serene and tranquil and full of peace."

I don't know how much of my story Peg took in, but when I finished, she nodded her head in her pillow in acknowledgment.

That night not only did I pull my curtain around my bed, but Peg's curtain around hers, joining them at the foot of our beds. And I lay in that curtained, two-personed world looking over at Peg from a pillow sopped with my tears, never having loved her more, never more uncertain of how long I would have her to love. *Please, God of the Parents Lounge, be with me*, I cried.

And He parted the curtains and stepped inside, and I lay in a curtained, three-personed world, and *everything was all right*.

18

*T*he next day when I woke up, Peg looked over at me with a shine of resurrection morning on her face.

"I feel better," she said, and asked me to raise her bed and arrange her pillows so she could sit up, no slumping over, so she could tell me a tale, no pausing for air.

I could not take it in.

"When I was so sick there, Mother," she said, as though talking of a time long past, "there were periods when my mind wouldn't focus on anything, when even my eyes wouldn't focus, and right during one of those times, this picture fell into my head. It was a cameo, ya know? Only not gold-rimmed—more like a picture in an old-fashioned fairytale book, only smudged around the edges. A picture of butterflies and bright sunshine and meadow flowers— like the ones from Jody," she added, pointing to the bunch of loosely arranged spring flowers dwarfed by the formal arrangements along the wall.

And then she did pause for breath before rushing on. "Do you think it was a gift, Mother? I mean, you know me. I hate to say God did something when maybe I did it myself, but all at once the picture just fell into my mind, and it was so vivid when everything else was so blurred. And my not being afraid to die, do you think that was a gift too? I always thought I'd be scared, but I wasn't at all, and it was like an acid test.

"I've been telling my friends about the cameo and it helping me not to be afraid, but I wanted to think about it more before I told you because you're skeptical too, when people say *God told me this* or *God did that.*"

"I have no doubt, Peggie, that your cameo was a gift from God."

But surely the cameo had come to prepare her for death. So why was she so much better?

"Yeah. It was kind of sad, though, that there were no people in it. If my subconscious had thought it up, it sure would have put people in it."

◇　◇　◇

When I see your cameo now, Peg, I see people in it. I see you, Peggie, running fleet of foot and never winded through the meadow grass to greet Mandy when she crossed over, and Jillian, and Mandy's brother, and Liz, and Ronnie and Tom and Jean and Josh.

John says that when he goes to bed at night, in addition to saying the Our Father, he says the Prayer for the Dead. Then he lists his grandparents' names, then yours. Then he tries to list the names of all the cystics he's known who have died, but he never gets to the end of the list.

The bright yellow drapes and the butterflies in your apartment couldn't compare with the bright sunshine that warmed your face or with the butterflies that lighted on your outstretched arms as you ran to welcome your friends, could they, Peg—as you rampaged through the flowers screaming their names?

◇　◇　◇

I prowled the halls then in my robe and slippers, hair uncombed, till I found Dr. Rathburn.

"She can't be feeling this much better," I mumbled through almost closed lips lest the aroma of unbrushed teeth waft his way. "She only started on ceftazidime yesterday afternoon."

"Studies show that some patients make marked improvement after one dose of ceftazidime."

But I could not believe.

Peg was sitting up again, talking to Jody on the phone when I got back to the room, talking for ever so long, but instead of being worn out when she hung up the phone, she was perked up.

"Jody said she wanted to call all week, but that she couldn't bring herself to because she knew something was terribly wrong. Then today she knew I was better, so she called today. Is that weird or what? She's going to think about living in the apartment across the hall."

Then a little later Peg's New York mother called and asked Peg what had been wrong, said that for so long she had wanted to call but couldn't because she knew something was very wrong.

"Nothing like that ever happens to me. How do they know these things?" Peg asked with mock exasperation. The phone calls surrounded what was happening to her with a mystical, unmistakable air.

"Weird how much better I feel than I did yesterday. I'm not makin' this up, ya know."

"I know, honey." And I did know. Everything that happened in Peg's five I-feel-better days happened in a misty bubble of hope. . . .

◊   ◊   ◊

Peg sitting in a lawn chair beside her bed when John visited that first afternoon. Peg saying, "I'm hungry, John."

John transfixed.

John scampering down the hall to get chicken soup from the refrigerator, heating it in the microwave, racing back with it like a puppy whose master, too long gone, has just come home.

Peg sipping her soup. Peg eating.

"Is it warm enough, Peggie? You'd like it a little warmer? I'll reheat it, Peggie. I won't be a minute, Peggie." The over-sized puppy skidding on the slippery floor.

Then both of us standing before her—we cannot sit— our mouths opening and closing with hers as she sips her soup, the woundedness that for so long has shadowed

John's face turning into wonder. Unspeakable.

Joe coming and finding Peg not sitting up in bed, not sitting beside her bed, but sitting in her wheelchair in front of the sink brushing her teeth.

Joe aghast. "Should she be . . . what happened, Meg?"

"I'm *better,* Father."

Peg insisting that her father come with us to the tub room while I wash her hair. "No, it can't wait till morning, Father. It's all right, Father. I'm *better.*"

Joe aglow.

I rubbing my knuckles sore because Peg's head can't get enough rubbing. "You missed a spot there, Mother. No, a little to the right, a little forward . . . ahh!"

Peg not getting a little better each day—but monumentally better each day.

Peg renting the color TV for *Fame,* sitting with John beside her bed, assigning me to the water mattress and roaring with laughter as I sink to rock bottom. How magical a time, Peg wanting me to have the water mattress, I munching popcorn as I watch TV over my head, John and Peg chatting during commercials—everything that happens, a happening.

Sandy coming on duty the next morning after several days off, not knowing what she will find.

Peg saying, "I have to use the bathroom, Sandy."

"You want me to help you to the potty chair, Peg?"

"No."

"You want a bedpan?"

"No."

Peg climbing unsteadily out of bed and soft-shoeing the yard or two to the bathroom.

Peg shooing me out to lunch with Jan at the Club Isabella, our wooden table rocking on the slanting, wide-paneled wooden floor. I unwinding in the old, artsy atmosphere, eating roast duckling without a trace of the bitter *What if Peggie dies while I'm gone?* seasoning.

Peg shooing Joe and me out to the Roman Villa for dinner.

"We've been here before, Joe. The movie's running backward, Joe." Joe and I lunging across the table for each other's hands and sobbing.

I stopped in Holy Rosary, and not a mass going on but a novena. I, not knowing what it is, only that the crowd is different—older women in black veils singing "O San Antonio, prego per me" in heavy Italian voices. I paying no mind, whispering private words of thanks to the God of the Parents Lounge. *Thank you, thank you, Father, for knowing what my daughter needed and for giving her the cameo. And thank you, thank you, thank you, Father, for how much better she's doing, and, as always, Father, thank you for the Parents Lounge and for the way you keep visiting me, even now again, Father.*

Peg talking and talking as though she's been filling up with talk all the days when she could not talk and is now unplugged.

"Everyone on the floor is watching the 'Miss America Pageant' tonight, Mother, yelling and screaming like the most important thing in the world is who's got the best measurements. Is that disgusting or what? I mean, nobody stops to think that what makes you great is not the prestige others give you, but the part of yourself you give away to others. I've stopped trying to explain it because nobody understands, not even the people you'd expect to understand. But you understand, right, Mother? I expect way back I got that from you, right, Mother?" Peg pretending exasperation again.

A couple from Bunting College who are looking after Peg's apartment bringing the long slip and jewelry Peg is again planning to wear when she is bridesmaid at Shelley's wedding—next week—in the future—Peg's future.

The couple saying, "We also brought this plaque, Peg. We searched your apartment for something we thought you'd like to have here before we decided on the plaque."

Department of Sunshine and Rainbows: Hopes Restored, Spirits Lifted, Enthusiasm Renewed.

Yes, oh, yes.

Peg saying, "Let's go through my insurance policies tonight, Mother. Even last week it was worryin' me that premiums might be due."

For three years Peg has accumulated all the insurance policies she can find that pay so much cash a day for every day you are in the hospital. Most of the policies have a one- or two-year waiting period for pre-existing conditions, so while she can support herself now on the policies already paying off, "wealth" is a year away.

"What do you think of this plan, Mother, when I start getting all my money? What if I give God ten percent off the top"—by *God* Peg meaning the church—"give myself ten percent to do something special with like buying furniture for my apartment or taking a trip, keeping what I need to live on, and giving the rest away? I've already told my friends to ask me for anything they need. I wouldn't tell everybody that, but the kind of friends I have won't ask unless they need it. Do you think ten percent is too much to splurge on myself?

"Ya know what I want you to do? Call up Ned—he's still the treasurer of the church, right?—and ask him how much it will cost to pave the church driveway. No, ask him about the driveway and the parking lot. I want to do the whole thing. Come on, Mother, you know how long the church has been wanting to pave the parking lot."

◇   ◇   ◇

The Domicron producing more humidity at night than during the day, and Peg drowning in it, calling Randy at Respiratory Therapy night after night to fix it. Randy giving Peggie his beeper number so she can call him directly. Peggie pondering what she can do for him in return. Maybe she can think of something original to say on the beeper.

And when next the waters rise, she dialing Randy's beeper. "420—gurgle, gurgle. 420—gurgle, gurgle."

"Do you think my message cheered him up, Mother?"

Randy walking into the room laughing, adjusting the Domicron and then bending low to Peg. "May I have this dance, Miss Woodson?" Randy holding out his arms as though holding her, waltzing around the dark bowery room.

Tears running down Peg's cheeks as her spirit rises from her bed and whirls, light as a spirit can be, in Randy's arms.

Peg, on the last of the five days, looking down at her legs and saying, "My muscles are atrophying here," and asking Angie to put extensions on her oxygen cord. And then standing to her feet, swaying to and fro, but still the great lady of the theater—"No, nobody help me"—walking across the room and—ta-da, ta-da—touching the far wall—with her elbow.

Joe and John and Angie and Mrs. Canfield and Mandy and I on our feet cheering and clapping, the nurses crowding in the doorway to watch.

Peg recovering from the grand march. I placing my hand on her leg, kissing her forehead.

Peggie saying, "Let's have a little independence here. You're pushing your mush limit, Mother."

I flitting down the hall. *Let's have a little independence here, Mother. Get your hand off my leg, Mother.* The words fluting in my heart. *You're pushing your mush limit, Mother.*

Was I ever in my lifetime so full of hope?

19

On the sixth ceftazidime morning, Peg said, "I don't feel any better today. But it's okay, Mother. The way things were before was not tolerable. This is tolerable."

I knew her lack of improvement bothered her, though, because later in the day she said, "Ya know how when something's bothering Father, but he doesn't know what it is, and he gets all tense until he does? Well, I've been like that all day, but now I know what's bothering me because every time I think of this one thing, I cry. . . . Oh, Mother, I'm afraid I'm going to be an invalid.

"And I keep trying to tell God that it will be okay if that's what He wants, but I can't get the words out. I mean, I've always given my life to God, so why can't I pray the prayer? Oh, Mother, I have always given my life to God."

That evening I heard Peg tell Angie that she'd tried all day to tell God it would be okay if she ended up an invalid, but that she knew it wouldn't count if she said the words and didn't mean them in her heart.

I could not help her, and that was the worst part for me. I did not know what to say to help her.

I told myself that Peg's not improving one day didn't mean she would not improve the next, did not mean she would get worse, but I felt myself closing down again lest panic fill me, its pressure crack me.

175

Peggie and *invalid* were contradictory terms. Peg had been given grace to accept death. Peg was not being given grace to accept invalidism. God gave only needed grace. . . .

◇　◇　◇

Life continued outwardly in the five *waiting* days, much as it had in the five *wonder* days.

Peg chased Joe and me out of the hospital again.

"Father's doin' so good these days, Mother. He's not tense or anything. I keep wondering what I could give you guys for your anniversary. . . . Hey, how about if I send both of you home together for the night?"

Joe and I went. Out to dinner and home for the night and out again for breakfast the next morning. I was anxious to get back to Peg by morning, but Joe said, "Come on, Meg, the Holiday Inn is on the way. You know it's your highest human pleasure to have breakfast at a Holiday Inn."

That time together was the best gift we'd been given on any of our twenty-nine wedding anniversaries—and it was Peggie's gift. Yet, while in the last five days we had viewed every brush stroke on the canvas of our lives with impressionist eyes, now details became surrealistically clear. Yes, Joe and I were able to leave Peg, but John had to stay with her to help get her ready for bed, and the floor had to hire an aide to be there for her in the night and to do the simplest getting-up things for her in the morning.

"Did Peggie give you a hard time about fixing her bed tray last night, John?"

"No, I don't think she's as hard on me as she is on you."

"You got it right?"

"I got it right." How pleased with himself John was.

◇　◇　◇

Once I went down to the refrigerator to get a plate of chicken and mashed potatoes Peg had had me stash away, but someone had gotten to it before me. The plate was there, covered with foil, but underneath lay nothing but chicken bones picked bare.

"It wouldn't be so bad if they'd done away with the plate

and all," Peg moaned, and, genuinely insulted, she reported the incident to Mary.

Mary said she knew who had taken Peg's food—a boy who was supposed to be fasting.

"Wimp!" snorted Peg, but after her initial indignation she told and retold her chicken-skeleton story with glee.

Last week I had heard only her laughter; this week I again heard her post-laughter coughing. This week I not only saw the thick green mucus she coughed up, but, streaked through it, the red blood. I thought of the Parents Lounge often, calling back the love and peace of the Parents Lounge.

Elizabeth, another longtime C.F. friend of Peg's, moved into Lucinda's bed during the beginning of the *lying-in-waiting* days. Liz laughed all hours of the day and night.

"Can you believe it, after all the other great people in this room, now Liz? Some *coincidence*, eh, Mother?"

Liz's carrot-red hair hung straight to her shoulders, and whenever Joe reviewed his Sunday sermon for Peg or had devotions with her, Liz scooted a chair close to us and plopped down, hair plopping up in the air.

"Do you mind if I join you?" she asked in the husky voice typical of cystics. "I don't know what I'd do without Jesus."

You could pick most cystics out of a crowd, with their stunted growth and skinny bodies, their rounded shoulders and sunken chests, the voices they proclaimed *sexy*, the happy-warrior look on their faces. I sat through a movie once all but sure that the boy in front of us had cystic fibrosis, wondering if his parents knew, if I should tell them. Later I got to know the family when the boy, Bobby, six years old, was in the hospital getting his C.F. lungs cleaned out.

Peg only had one fault to find with Liz. Liz had gotten her driver's license on her sixteenth birthday a year ago, but then refused to drive, having her mother take her everywhere. So Peg's delight in seeing her friend was heightened when she learned that this time Liz had heeded Peg's nagging and driven herself to the hospital.

"I have freed a friend from the dreaded reliance on

mother," Peg crowed—to her mother.

One day Josh, another old C.F. friend, came in down-stairs for a checkup and then, in the habit of C.F.ers, up to the fourth to see who was in. Josh had watched his brother die of C.F. back in Montana, had heard about the C.F. Center here and hopped a plane by himself to get here, his parents unwilling to extend themselves to get the care he needed. He had arrived at Cleveland Hopkins Airport, a miniature seventeen-year-old coughing his insides out, stopping strangers in the rush to baggage claim till he found one who explained to him how to take the Rapid Transit to University Circle and then the bus to Rainbow Babies and Children's Hospital.

C.F.ers all had stories that would break your heart, but C.F. rarely broke them.

◊   ◊   ◊

Peg continued to worry that what we were putting John through should be a good experience for him, and one night when he came in bushed, going on about the stress at work getting to him, Peg said, "You know, John, your job is not the most important thing in your life." The time to speak out had come.

"I know, Peggie."

And then, as Peggie told me later, "I ruined it, Mother, I couldn't resist. I said, 'The most important thing in your life is *me.*' " Peggie never stopped aching to be someone's number-one friend—even when she was.

◊   ◊   ◊

This chapter isn't going anywhere, Peggie. Of course, the five days it's about didn't go anywhere either. But I think I'm avoiding talking about certain things that happened in the hospital in those suspended-in-time days because I'm avoiding getting angry at you. All your life I treated you with kid gloves, Peggie, lest I make life more difficult for you than it was with your C.F.

◊   ◊   ◊

"Whatever happened to Tom and Jean?" I asked Peg, referring to two cystics whose parents had given them up shortly after birth when they discovered the infants had C.F. Tom and Jean had ended up in separate foster homes, seeing each other only when their hospitalizations coincided. "I never forgot how you told me they cling to each when they meet in the hospital, Peg."

"Well, Tom turned eighteen and the state wouldn't pay his foster parents to keep him anymore, and he never worked, so he couldn't get disability, so he's on welfare living in a room by himself. I feel sad about that. I guess Jean is still in her foster home. I haven't seen her in a while."

◇　◇　◇

Did you ever think, Peggie, that some mothers did a worse job with their C.F.ers than I did? At least I never gave you away. We moved to Cleveland so you could get the best care available.

The other day I asked John if there was anything you and he talked about in the hospital when you were alone together that I should know about for this book, Peg, and he said that every day, as soon as I left the room, you exploded about how you wanted things done in a certain way, and why oh why couldn't I get your bed tray right the first time?

He also told me about the day in the five waiting-to-see days when he took you for a ride in your wheelchair and stopped in a deserted hallway by a big window and you sat looking out into the night and cried, something you never did in front of him. "I think I'm going crazy," you sobbed. "I have this really weird feeling of wanting my mother in the hospital and not wanting her here at the same time. I have to get out of the hospital. I have to get away from my mother."

How could you, Peggie?

John said he patted your shoulder and promised he'd take you out in his car far from the hospital, that you got excited about that and stopped crying.

Angie says it's not that dying patients don't want their parents to be there; they don't want them to have to be

there. Well . . . small comfort, Peggie. Did you ever think
there might have been times in the hospital when I'd had it
with you? Well, there weren't, Peggie. Taking care of you in
the hospital was my vocation. Yet I gave you space to be
alone with your friends, alone with yourself, and I did my
dead-level best every single night to get your blasted bed
tray right.

Angie says that no matter what peace patients make
with their dying, they still feel an underlying anger. They
have to pick someone to be angry at, and they pick the one
they can trust to keep on loving them no matter what.

Angie also says that when you're dying, someone trying
their hardest on your behalf isn't good enough, and that you
were a perfectionist even before you were dying.

Angie's so wise, Peggie, but . . . get lost, sweet reason. I
want to be mad.

You were critical of me even as a child, and the older
you got, the more critical and demanding you got. You specialized in pointing out my faults, but never saw your own.
Ben says I should have called you on that—that you
couldn't take responsibility for faults you weren't aware of,
and had you taken responsibility for them, you'd have been
more in control of yourself, more approving of yourself, and
less disapproving of me.

You hurt me almost beyond bearing lots of times, Peggie.
I know your C.F. gave you a hard way to go. Well, it didn't
exactly make my life easy. . . .

Well, I got that out of my system, didn't I? I guess if I
can get that angry at you and love you as much as I do—
because I love you as much as I do—I ought to be able to
accept your anger along with your love. But, still. . . .

I've finished the first course in my counseling program.
Going back to school was harder than I anticipated. I'm not
sure I want to keep struggling that hard to keep up.

One thing I was saving to tell you at the end of this book
was that I kept my deathbed promise to you—that I went
on a diet. Well, I did lose weight, but I've gained most of it
back. Life isn't as pat as we'd like it to be. Suffering doesn't
always change us in the ways we plan for it to change us.

Sometimes I'm not sure I want to keep on struggling this hard to survive.

The nice things you said in the hospital, Peg, when you acted like you liked having me around—Isn't my mother doin' good? . . . It's good to have you here, Mother. . . . I think we could live together again, Mother—*were they all an act?*

20

*T*he Domicron continued to produce noses-full of moisture at night, and though they tried, in response to repeated phone calls from Respiratory Therapy, the Domicron people could not determine why.

Finally Angie and Peggie figured out that the thermostat on the cord from the Domicron nestled into Peg's body more at night than it did during the day and thus reacted to her body temperature rather than the temperature of the room, increasing its output of humidity accordingly.

They took the cardboard circle from inside a roll of adhesive tape, fastened it over the thermostat so it couldn't rest on her body, and—presto—no humidity problem.

"Was that a technical breakthrough or what, Father? At the very least the company should give me a machine to use in my apartment when I go home, don't you think?"

Every time Respiratory Therapy talked to Domicron, the Domicron people asked how Peggie was doing.

"It's like they know me, Father. There's a lot of nice people out there."

One night Peg asked me to take her exploring in the hospital attached to Rainbow, "Where, Mother, they post all kinds of interesting and funny notices."

Peg read notice after notice till she came on one advertising for people to live in the hospital to participate in a medical experiment. "Oh, Mother, didn't I tell you this was a fun place to come? Just read this. Can't you see some poor souls responding to this ad but not reading the fine print and discovering once they were in that all their food would be fed to them through their noses? We're preoccupied with noses these days, aren't we, Mother?"

It took some doing to find places to go in the hospital to make you laugh, but Peg managed. Who would have dreamed that our last mother-daughter excursion would be to read an advertisement for people willing to be fed through their noses?

Peg went on one other excursion, when John took her for the promised ride in his car. He put a second tank of oxygen in the front seat, and she made the transition, but when they got back and the nurses were fussing over her, I asked John how she had done.

"Okay at first. She waved her hands around like she does and cried, 'Trees, trees! People, people!' But in a few minutes the movement of the car wore her out. It was worth it, though, she was so glad to get away from the hospital."

"We kept having adventures, Mother," Peg said when she'd rested. "Like we stopped in front of this field in Gates Mills, and there was a border of trees around it, and it was raining, and then right while we were sitting there, the sun came out. It reminded me of my cameo with the border around the field and all. I've never seen air so fresh and clear.

"And then a man and his daughter came into the field with a horse, and they put it through its paces. I mean, what are the odds that we'd stop in front of a field like that? And John played John Michael Talbot's 'The Last Supper' on his stereo going and coming.

"You remember that other time, John, when you took me out of the hospital in your car, in your old Volkswagen, and the window on my side was out and you had it taped closed with gray plastic, and all of a sudden this black smoke came billowing into the car, and I started coughing, and you reached across me and punched your fist through the plastic, and we were driving down Euclid Avenue with this smoke pouring out of the car and my head stuck through the hole in the plastic."

Usually I left the room when Peg and John talked, or if I stayed, they talked as though I had left the room. Now while they looked at each other, I had the feeling they were talking for my benefit. A good feeling.

"You never did know the part about my coughing from the black smoke, did you, Mother?" Peg asked smugly.

"And then, John, when we got back to the hospital, remember how Liz's parents were here and they said, 'We were driving down Euclid, Peggie, past this little Volkswagen filled with black smoke, and we said "Look at that dog sticking his head out through the hole in the window," and then we looked again and said, "That's no dog. That's Peggie." ' "

"I may not have known about the smoke, Peg," I said when they had undoubled themselves from their laughter, "but I did know that John spent the night in the hospital because I had to drive over the next morning with eight quarts of oil for his car. I remember thinking, *They've spent the night together. I don't have to worry about Peg being compromised anymore.*" I said it smugly in return for Peg's smugness, knowing she would be embarrassed.

We floated close together, John and Peg and Joe and I, in a silvery pool of calm through those five still-waiting-to-see days, but, at least in my ears, with the roar of Dead Man's Falls downriver. Would she fly over the edge or not, this young woman? My young woman. My youth. My caretaker in my old age.

It was easier knowing, I cried. But wasn't sure. Was. Was sure she would die in the end. Not sure. Not. . . .

The pain rose steadily from the back of my neck up and over my head and down into my eyes. Every day the same pilgrimage.

During one of her father's visits, Peg talked to him about her inability to accept invalidism, and he talked to her about her purpose in life being to glorify God in whatever state she found herself. And she smacked her head with her palm and said, "Oh, how could I have forgotten that? I've always known that. And with the quotation and all. I mean, if I'm in bed I can glorify God. If I'm not in bed, I can glorify God. Do you sense a breakthrough coming here, Mother?"

But the breakthrough didn't come.

For once I did not want to think about the quotation.

◇   ◇   ◇

Peggie finally conceded that she would not be able to be bridesmaid at Shelley's wedding.

"Oh, Mother, the first time in my life I can't make myself do something I really want to do."

But then Shelley came to visit two days before the wedding, all the way up from Columbus, bringing Peg a present for being in the hospital, and a bridesmaid's present, but mostly the present of herself.

"Hi, Pallie," Peg cried in delight when Shelley stuck her head inside the door.

"Hi, Pallie," Shelley cried back with the slightest tremor in her voice. "How's my best pallie?"

As magically improved as Peg seemed to those of us who had been with her at her worst, how must she look to someone who hadn't seen her since they'd trekked together from the Bunting campus through the field beyond the Student Center, over a fence, and on a half mile to Taco Bell?

When I walked Shelley to the elevator, she told me that just before Peg went into the hospital, she had called long distance and told Shelley about a wonderful quotation she'd gotten from her minister.

"Get a pencil and paper, Shelley," she said. "I know you're going to want to write this down."

"I've carried the card I wrote the quotation on in my wallet all this time, Mrs. Woodson. I've had a lot of pressure in my life lately with graduating from college and finding a job and an apartment and getting married all at once. And with Peggie—" she added, looking, woebegone, back at Peggie's room. "And I keep taking the card out to read."

And she took the card out of her wallet to show me, smudged and limp but with the words legible: *Endurance is not just the ability to bear a hard thing, but to turn it into glory.*

And, again, I *knew*. The quotation *had* been given to Peggie to guide her on her last great adventure. Peggie was going to die. Was. Was.

It was terrible.

"If the ceftazidime's not working anymore, Dr. Rathburn, why not try something else?" I mean, what if the inevitable could be postponed a bit?

I felt ancient of days and everlastingly sad, but I was in contact with reality again, and I also felt invincible.

Shelley phoned on the morning of her wedding. "Can you imagine, Mother, on the morning of her wedding day? She says I'm listed as a part of the wedding party in the program, but with an asterisk after my name, and that down at the bottom it says *honorary bridesmaid*. And she put a rose on the altar in my place. The program doesn't say what the rose is for, but Shelley says she knows, and a few people who matter know.

"Oh, Mother, the first time I haven't been able to do something I really—" She buried her face in the pillow she'd been leaning over and, like a car running out of gas, her body bucked with her sobs.

When had she started leaning over her pillow again?

Angie had been keeping Peg's bridesmaid gown in her apartment, and she brought it in that day and hung it over the rail at the foot of Peggie's bed. Everyone oohed and aahed over the gown, but it was too much for me—that rosy, gauzy, empty creation swaying slightly as the door to the room opened and solid people breezed past.

◊　◊　◊

Perhaps Peg's final rush downstream began on the last of the *floating* days . . . I wonder . . . because Mandy and Liz both moved out of the room that day.

Mandy said a friend had moved into a two-bed room down the hall, a friend she had solemnly promised she would room with the next time they were in together. Mrs. Canfield said there was so much noise in our room at night with people talking over the sound of the Domicron that

Mandy never got enough sleep, and I knew both these things were true.

But I wondered if either was the real reason for Mandy's leaving. If I'd been Mrs. Canfield, I'd have gotten Mandy out of there a long time ago.

Never would I forget the sight of Mandy riding high on her bed as they wheeled her out of the room, hands covering her limp-flower face, tears spurting out between her fingers.

Sandy called me into the hall to tell me Liz was leaving too. She said that Liz wanted us to know how bad she felt, but that she had roomed with so many people who had died, she could not go through it again. She would be back, she promised, every day to spend quality time with Peg.

And she was. Mandy and Mrs. Canfield and Liz continued to be with us in every way that mattered.

But what with Peg's empty gown hanging over her bed and the empty space where Mandy's bed had been, I was relieved to have Jan take me up the hill beyond Little Italy to a Greek restaurant, and then farther up the hill to a convent of cloistered, Carmelite sisters.

Someone at the Jesuit Retreat House had suggested that I talk to Sister Mary of the Holy Spirit at the convent concerning the maintaining of God's presence in my life, but a mere mortal talking to someone named Sister Mary of the Holy Spirit?

No, Jan and I just absorbed the peace of the convent grounds, and I told her that if I lost not only Peg but, in time, Joe, and my worst fear came true and I belonged to no one on earth, I would still have Someone to whom I belonged. That I was going to devote my life to living in the Presence of the God of the Parents Lounge and to helping other people realize that, more than anything else, they wanted to live in the Presence of God, too.

I was glad for the timing of this talk with Jan because when we got back to the hospital, Peg's gown was gone, Liz and Mandy and all their belongings were gone, both their beds made up with white hospital spreads pulled so tight a Mother Superior could have bounced a quarter on them.

The silence and whiteness of the room immobilized me

in the doorway. Someone had lowered the curtain on stage 420 while I was gone, rearranged the props, and raised the curtain on a scene so sterile that it could be nothing but the setting for the final act.

"It's going to be worse—this time—Mother," Peg said, "because—this time I know—what it's like."

21

*F*ive days of falling in one night.

In one night, while I slept, Peg hurtled all the way down-river, over the falls, and onto the crying-out rocks of pain and sweat and weakness and gasping-for-air below.

It was worse this time, the pain and sweat . . . the *persecution* of it all. *Not again,* Peg's eyes begged mine.

I could not meet her eyes. I could not help her. It was not like Peg to beg for help. *Dear God, we can't go through this again.*

Two friends from Bunting were due to visit Peg that Thursday, the first of her five last days.

"Shall I call and ask them not to come, Peggie?"

"No. Go—up to five—Mother—and get—the lightest—top you can find. I want—to change—my top—before—they get here. Why—is it—so hot?"

On my way to five I darted into a phone booth to tell my mother in Florida that the end for Peg was near. I dreaded what the news might do to her damaged heart. I could not lose my daughter and my mother at the same time. Yet I did not talk long. I had a lightweight top to find on five.

"You call *this*—a lightweight—top—Mother? Can I—have another—zomax yet—Mother?"

"I felt every top up there, Peggie. This one really did feel the lightest." My hands fumbled the bottle as I tapped out a zomax, and pills went rolling. I scurried down the hall for fresh water. Crawled under the bed searching out every precious zomax tablet. Bumped my head on the bed springs. Put my hands over my head under the bed and groaned.

It was symbolic of Peg's five last days, my curling into my anguish under the bed and calling back the God of the Parents Lounge. *I know you're here, God,* I said, and He was under the bed with me. I loved Him more than I could say, and He loved me—more than I could say.

Peggie's on her way to you, I told Him, tears puddling on the floor. I could no longer hold her back from such love. *Get ready, heaven. Peggie's on her way.*

Peg spent all her time collapsed over her bed tray or her bed rail again, potty chair beside her bed again, straight-backed sentinel to her indignities. Infirmities.

When her friends arrived, I cautioned them about how they would find her, but they came out of her room shaken to the core of their young adult souls. Still, they hugged me and asked how I was doing and said they would pray for me. I hoped Peg's friends knew how much their attempts at comfort did comfort, though I sensed that their efforts seemed inadequate to them.

The Lerneys visited, too, that Thursday, leaning far over Peg in their desire to ease her way. The last visitors Peg was aware of having. Except for John, who wasn't considered a visitor.

"Don't come tomorrow—John," Peg would say. "You have—your job. You have—to study."

"Okay," said John, but when tomorrow came, so did John.

"Come on—John—I want—your solemn promise—that you will not—come tomorrow."

"I promise," said John.

"And especially—on Memorial Day—John. You know how—the Byrne clan—gathers—on Memorial Day. Promise—you won't come—on Memorial Day."

What would we have done had John kept his promises?

John and Peg and I watched *Fame* together that last Thursday night, watched Coco flutter like a butterfly reaching for her dream. When the program was over, Peg heard her father's footsteps coming down the hall.

"I wonder—what he'll—talk to me—about—that will be—just right—for today," she said.

And then, "How can—I have a—dream—Father—if I'm not going—to get—better?"

Her father talked to her about the apostle Paul writing his letter to the Philippians from prison and saying that his dream was to be like Jesus, and that it was in this letter, written from prison, that Paul said, "I have learned in whatever state I am to be content."

Peggie had dozed on and off that day, groggier than she'd yet been, and the nurses had put the sides on her bed up for the first time in the daytime.

"Oh, no—Father's—struck again. I mean—with these bars—on my bed—and me—feelin' all day—like I was—in prison. It's always—been the—aim of my life—to be—like Jesus. How—could I—forget?" And she smacked her head. "I can be—like Jesus—if I stay—in bed—or if—I get—out of bed. This will—make it easier—to say—the prayer—about—bein' an invalid.

"You remember—my favorite Bible verse—when I was—in high school—John? 'Whatever is true—whatever is noble—whatever is pure—whatever is lovely—think about—these things'? Well—Paul wrote—that—in prison—too."

◇   ◇   ◇

Of Friday, the second of Peg's last five days, I remember little. Except that Father Joe, my favorite priest from the Jesuit Retreat House, called and said that forty people who were at the house on a thirty-day retreat were praying for Peggie. I cried when I hung up, but on the phone I had sounded unresponsive.

And I remember that Mandy and Mrs. Canfield came to call, and that Liz kept dropping in to rub Peggie's back. And that Angie kept being assigned to us. And that that day and every day Peg piped in a tiny voice, "Oh—Angie—I'm so glad—you're here."

And that day and every day Liz motioned me into the hall and asked, "Why is this happening, Mrs. Woodson?"

I knew she was asking not just for Peg but for all her C.F. friends who had died, and for herself, but none of my theological discourses satisfied her.

Then on Friday night I read to Peg from *Abandonment to Divine Providence* and called Liz in from the hall. Strange how effortlessly you come to love someone you take care of spiritually. "If we only have sense enough to leave everything to the guidance of God's hand we should reach the highest peak of holiness."

"You mean you don't know why these things are happening, Mrs. Woodson?"

"No, Liz, I don't know."

"Me neither," said Liz, and didn't ask me *why* again.

But the main thing I remember about the last Friday was that Joe and John came to *know* along with me, and that Angie acknowledged the *knowing* I suspect she'd had for some time.

Joe and John and Angie and Dr. Rathburn all *knew* that Peggie would die. It depleted my energy not having anyone's *not-knowing* to fight against. I was so tired on Friday that I worried about *my* health. *How could I?*

I knew that everyone else *knew* on Friday because of the comments they made—that even Peggie all but *knew*.

John to me: "If I didn't know all of this would have an end for Peggie and everything would be all right for her, I would go crazy."

Joe to me: "Thank you for being Joey's and Peggie's mother."

Angie to me: "Peggie and I talked from midnight till three o'clock this morning. It was a very special time for me because . . . anyway, just before I left, Peggie said, 'You know what it feels like when somebody hugs you? Imagine what it will feel like when Jesus hugs you.'"

Peggie to Dr. Rathburn: "You know—when I first knew— I was supposed—to be—an editor? When I started—editing—people's conversations—in my head."

Dr. Rathburn to me: "I used to lose them in childhood. Now I lose them on the edge of their becoming."

Joe to Peggie: "If I had a choice, Peggie, between having healthy children and having two children with C.F., I'd choose you and Joey any day."

Joe to Peggie: "You're everything as a daughter I could want."

Peggie to Joe: "When Dr. Rathburn—came back—from Kansas City—he asked me—if I wanted—to fight—and I had—such a reputation—as a fighter—to uphold—I said I did—but I'm—not sure—if I—really—want to go on—like this—or just—go to heaven—now."

Peggie to Dr. Rathburn: "I don't—want to get—all mushy—or anything—but I—want to tell you—that I'm—not afraid—to die. I thought—it would help—you—to know that."

Dr. Rathburn to Peggie: "Okay."

Peggie to Joe and John and Angie and Dr. Rathburn and me as we stood around her bed on Friday night: "This would—make a great—picture—ten years—from now."

22

*T*hursday gone. Friday gone. Where have they gone? Is it morning yet? When Saturday is gone, will Peggie, too, be gone?

Open your eyes, Meg. Turn your head. Look at your daughter.

I turning my head. Looking. My daughter lying flat and still.

No! It can't be! Not while I was sleeping!

I tearing free from a twist of sheets, falling to my knees at Peggie's side. Looking. Touching.

She's breathing, Meg. She's warm.

Oh, God. Oh, God.

I toppling into a chair by her bed, holding my robe with its insides toward me and poking my arms into the sleeves, tucking the front of the robe behind me. *Nobody can see behind me. Joe gave me my robe for Christmas. I love my soft, furry, blue robe.*

I keeping watch by Peggie's side. A solitary early morning watch in a solemn room.

Peg screaming.

What is this? What's happening? Her screams freezing my flesh.

Mary and Sandy and Georgie running from every direction. "Mary's here, Peggie. You're okay. Mary's here." Each one stroking an arm, a leg. "Georgie's here, Peggie. Everything's all right."

"We're going to start her on a morphine drip, Mrs. Woodson, to relax her central nervous system."

"But Peggie always said . . . all the C.F. patients say . . . morphine hastens death."

"No, Mrs. Woodson, not in the small amounts we'll give it to her." The nurses stroking my body as it sits bowed in its chair.

Peggie quieted, back with us from wherever she has been, being helped from her bed. Weighed.

How can they do this to her?

They have to weigh her, Meg. Water retention, remember?

I know, I know. But, it's too late. *How can they?*

"Eighty-eight pounds—is okay—Mother. I've been—lots thinner—than that. As long as—I don't go—under—eighty-five."

She's going to die undefeated, Meg.

Yes. Undefeated, Peggie. Shine, Peggie. Turn it into glory.

"You don't look that thin, Peggie, not even your arms." She doesn't. They don't. She looks ethereal, but not rickety. I dry-sobbing with joy that Peggie is not going to die too thin and that I can reassure her.

She still needs you, Meg.

Peg, too weak to brush her teeth, wiping her mouth with a flavored sponge on a stick.

"Do you—think—my potassium level—is making me—this weak—Mother? Ya know—I think—" Silence. "What was—I saying—Mother?" Silence. "Ya know—Mother—I think—you and I—"

You and I what, Peggie? What?

I will never know what.

Liz showing me how to press my hands into Peg's back when she coughs, and this support helping Peg. I leaping up every time Peg coughs, pressing my hands into her back. At last, at last, helping Peggie when she coughs.

◇　　◇　　◇

Mandy going home. Mandy unexpectedly improved.

Mrs. Canfield leaving her in her little wheelchair beside Peg's bed to say good-bye.

Mandy, face alight, bringing out present after good-bye present hidden under a towel on her lap. Butterfly napkins. Rainbow stickers. And then, next to last, a box of goldfish food. And then, and then, swimming about in a little bowl, a goldfish.

Mandy worrying because the fish isn't lively.

"Don't worry—Mandy—we'll name him—Fishy—and he'll have—to live up—What was I—saying—live up—to what other fish—expect a fish—named Fishy—to be."

Oh, Peggie, shine.

"It's to keep you company when I'm gone, Peggie." Mandy desperate that Peggie understand, but her voice barely audible now, her eyes turning and returning to the door.

Somebody get her out of here.

Mrs. Canfield coming in and squeezing my hand. I remembering how she squeezed my hand on my first night in the hospital as we stood in the darkened hallway and filled our daughters' vaporizers side by side. *I don't think Mandy's going to make it this time.*

I don't think Peggie's going to make it this time either.

"Good-bye, Mrs. Canfield. Thanks for everything. Good-bye, Mandy."

Live long, little one. Be happy.

The room silent again without them. *Soon. We must find a cure for this damned disease soon.*

Peggie screaming again. Wave after wave of primitive screams. It sounds like terror. Peggie, fists clenched, body rigid but vibrating with the force of her screams. It looks like terror.

The nurses running in. I squeezing in between them, staking out my spot of leg to stroke. "It's okay, Peggie. Mother's here."

They increasing her morphine drip.

I not asking but knowing they are hastening her death.

The room tilting.

"Stay—with her—for a minute—Sandy." Why am *I* talking in fits and starts?

I stumbling into the doctor in the hall. "Death stinks, Dr. Rathburn."

The doctor nodding. "I've lost Peggie by a hair's breadth, but if I'd saved her this time, we'd have gone through the same thing six months down the road."

I back in the room. Peg sitting up in bed, looking vacantly around the vacant room. "Where—is everybody? Oh—what a way—to go."

It's okay, Meg. It's good that Peggie—

Oh, shut up. Please.

Peg lying down, sitting up, looking vaporous, cloudborne, but not vacant. "Tell Father—to bring—my will. I need—to sign it. Tell Father—he can have—communion now."

Shine, Peggie, shine.

She was right when she said that cystics always knew.

I was right when I said that she'd make the acknowledgment when the time came.

I phoning our house—crying—phoning the church—crying, unable to locate Joe. *I don't need this.* Phoning parishioners' houses, finally finding him. "You better come now, Joe. This could be the day."

I remembering John's request that he be with Peg at the end, locating him at work. "It could be today, John."

Peg leaning back against her pillows, face splotchy-gray, hair in dark greasy ringlets, eyes darting from corner to corner of the room calling forth unnamed foes. Woes.

Help, somebody. Somebody come soon. Time passing.

I hearing long legs thudding down the hall, knowing it is John. He slamming to a stop in the door of room 420, hair awry, jacket half off one shoulder, clutching a book in both hands.

John sitting on the edge of Peg's bed. "Remember how we planned to take a trip to an inn in Maine when I graduated, Peggie? You remember, Peg, an old inn on the rocky coast of Maine? Well, listen to this." The book opening of itself to its appointed place. "Land's End Inn, built 1863,

White Harbor, Maine, ocean view."

He knows it is too late. She knows it is too late. Each knows the other knows it is too late, but it is a consummate act of love, John holding his book close to Peg's face so she can see his offering shining through the mist. Peg leaning back against her pillows, listening to the ocean thunder, thunder, thunder on the rocky coast of Maine.

I scuttling from the room lest I be blinded by the ocean light.

Joe checking into Ronald McDonald House. I needing him here. Wanting him here. But wanting Peggie to myself too.

Peg sitting up. "No—don't hold me." Peg signing her will in crooked old-woman's script.

I never imagined such a day.

Joe serving communion. "This is My body that was broken for you. Do this in remembrance of Me." Joe's voice breaking as it broke when he spoke those words nine years ago in the room—wherever—to Joey.

Dr. Rathburn telling us Peg has developed liver problems, heart problems.

Angie coming on duty.

"Oh—Angie—I'm so glad—you're here."

Angie motioning us into the hall and asking us—as Peggie's nurse having to ask us—"I have to ask you, Reverend and Mrs. Woodson, if you want Peggie resuscitated should she go into heart arrest."

John standing behind us. "No," he blurts before and for us all.

They're so young, John and Angie, so good and so strong. Will they be young when this is over? I unable to tell them what they mean to me.

"How does—my hair look—Mother?"

Joe leaving for the night. "You know that you'll have a resurrected body, don't you, Peggie?"

"Well—of course—Father." Indignation. "I am—a Calvinist—you know."

Joe and I holding each other in the hall, laughing and crying.

Joe going back to Peg. "I'd give my life for you, Peggie, and God loves you far more than I."

Peggie wanting my cot moved so it touches her bed, but two I.V. poles and the potty chair blocking my side of her bed, and the Domicron and the table with John's stereo equipment the other.

Derek sending off for a six-foot extension cord, and he and John rearranging every item around Peg's bed till every inch of space is filled, but the cot fits.

Peg surveying the scene. "It makes me—claus—tro—phobic."

John and Derek moving everything back. "No problem, Peggie."

"Read to me—out of—your handbook—Mother."

I keeping lonely late-night watch at Peggie's side, not reading from my handbook. "These are words Jesus spoke, Peggie, as a young man when He faced His death. 'For this hour I was born, and for this hour I came into the world.' "

Peg hanging over her bed rail toward my cot. "I don't—think—anybody—appreciates—how hard I'm tryin'—to make—the glory."

I wondering if I would give my life to save her. Yes, if she would live long. Yes, if she would live well. No, if. . . .

What kind of unmother am I?

"Is it time—to send—another month's—rent—on my—apartment—Mother?" She too groggy to know what she is saying, the morphine doing its numbing, dumbing work.

Don't, Peggie. No more, Peggie.

Peg sleeping. I falling into my cot.

A social worker coming into the room, a new, substitute Child Life Worker Peg has told me about. "He gives new meaning—to the word *burly,* but you love him—right away. They say—he's an unemployed steel worker—and a boun-cer—at rock concerts."

He sitting in Peg's wheelchair and walking it over to the cot. "The first week Peggie was in, Mrs. Woodson, I was showing a movie down on three, and along came this little patient in a little wheelchair, being pushed by a big patient in a big wheelchair, being pushed by a mother. A regular wagon train. It was a kid's movie, and I could tell Peg was only there for Mandy, the way she kept laughing so loud and poking Mandy to laugh. Your daughter is quite a person, Mrs. Woodson."

The burly stranger leaning over and kissing my cheek. I feeling tucked in.

Was there ever a night when I so needed to be tucked in by a bouncer such as he?

Saturday—gone.

23

Sunday morning.

I waking slowly on purpose. Head emerging from the covers, head disappearing beneath the covers.

I half-dreaming. I, an artist, smocked, poised on a platform suspended from the ceiling in the middle of the room. A slender angel-artist complete with canvas and wing-ed palette capturing for eternity the scene below—the curtained alcove in the uninhabited land.

I painting the desolate land—the metal beds, empty; the slatted lawn chairs, empty; the tables and cabinets, bare; the walls stripped. No get-well cards. No rock star posters. I painting everything on a slant, everything in shades of gray.

I peering down inside the alcove from my swing high up in the air, the beds close enough that if the mother in one and the daughter in the other each reached out a hand, they could touch. But how can I paint such private space, the feeling the mother feels as she turns her head toward her daughter, as she reaches out her hand, as her hand dangles midway?

I throwing paint on canvas with frenzied strokes—everything in the alcove in celestial white—curtains, beds, wheelchair, lawn chair, potty chair, I.V.s—everything in celestial white—but the mother and daughter in shades of beige—golden, glowing beige radiating all the way from bed to bed.

But how can I paint the only sound in the room, the rough, drawing-in sound of the daughter's breathing? The artist, covering her ears, slashing an X in black across the daughter's chest, but in eradicating the sound, eradicating the daughter, the alcove, the artist . . . .

I tearing out of bed and down to the kitchen so I will have fresh water for Peg should she need it. Dropping her cup, bending to pick it up, and hearing Peg scream. It is worse from a distance. I freezing in my bent position, head up, face fixed in recoil.

An aide pushing a cart of bed linen, a nurse carrying I.V. tubing and bottle, a young boy returning jauntily from the shower, red hair slicked back—can it be Ronnie, or Lonnie?—all stopped in their tracks, a movie stuck in mid-frame, the look of nightmare in fluorescent hospital daylight contorting every face.

The movie starting again, in fast speed. I running with the rest.

"I know how it sounds to you, Mrs. Woodson, but Peggie's hallucinating." Angie. "Hallucinating that you're being torn to bits by mad wolves is nothing like being torn to bits by mad wolves. She has no memory of it now."

She'll have no memory of anything soon the way they keep increasing her morphine, increasing her oxygen.

You don't know that, Meg.

I do so know that. I learned it with Joey. Don't tell me I don't know what I know.

I calling John. "I think it will be today, John."

John worrying that the responsibility for getting him there at the right time is adding to my burdens.

Joe phoning our funeral director. He cut short his vacation to come home when Joey died. You don't forget something like that. Joe phoning Peg's beloved Pastor Arthur. We agreeing that she would want him to conduct her funeral. Joe caving in against the wall.

◊　◊　◊

"Here's a copy of my monthly newsletter, Mrs. Wood-son." Dr. Rathburn. "I always gave Peggie the first copy. If she said it was okay, it was okay. . . . I'm going to miss talking to her." A sentimental speech for Dr. Rathburn.

"Dr. Rathburn says he knows you can't read this, Peggie, but he wants you to have the first copy of his newsletter anyway."

Peg nodding, always having loved her doctor, accepting this evidence that he loves her back.

I happy that she is aware enough to look as gratified as she looks. I grieving for her doctor's grief.

Friends coming and sitting with us for hours. Just being with us.

Peg drifting in and out of consciousness.

◇　◇　◇

Midafternoon.

I not knowing where the day has gone. I drifting in and out of full consciousness of where I am and what is happening.

Loud crashing in the hall. Shouts. Glass breaking. Shattering us all into alertness.

"What—what's that—what's that?"

"Lonnie's back, Peg. Lonnie by himself. He was riding down the hall on his I.V. pole and collided with Sandy-with-med-tray."

"Jerk!"

"Oh, I don't know. Joey used to ride down the hall on his I.V. pole."

"Yeah—but Joey—was no jerk."

Peggie's ever-Pegginess relieving our tension. All of us laughing all out of proportion.

"I think she has a little time yet, Reverend and Mrs. Woodson." Dr. Rathburn.

John and I slipping down to the cafeteria, sipping Pepsis at an outdoor table in the sun.

I crazy-desperate for a future, overstepping my bounds. "It's my fantasy, John, that you and Angie will get married one day and let me be a grandmother to your children." I scared all out of proportion that I have lost John the way I always lost Peggie when I tried too hard to keep her.

"You can be grandmother to my children no matter who I marry, Mrs. Woodson. I could never go through this with someone and not always have them be a part of my life."

Bless John.

"I try to make myself feel better about Peggie by thinking that she isn't my *true love*, you know, the woman I'd marry. But now I realize that what we have is every bit as important as that kind of love, if not more so. . . . I can't believe this is really happening. . . ."

I thinking, *There is no comfort for any of us anywhere,* but then thinking, *There is comfort for me sitting here in the sun listening to John confide in me.*

The afternoon passing. Where? How?

Peg talking rhythmically, compulsively twisting the tube coming from her broviac. I holding her hands. She, with unbelievable strength, wresting them away, twisting, twisting every tube entering or exiting her body.

"You mustn't pull out your broviac, honey."

She fondling my face.

That must be the best feeling in the world, Meg.

Maybe she can't see. Maybe she's comforting herself with the feel of my face.

Peg jamming her fingers up my nose.

I cannot get her fingers out of my nose. I cannot bear to lose her with her fingers up my nose.

Peg afraid to sleep. "Can't sleep. Can't sleep. Now this—is important. I'm past—the point—where I can—make a decision—about whether—I live—or die—and you know Sandy—Father—Sandy—my nurse today. Well—Sandy's so—efficient—what was I saying—Sandy's so efficient—I'm afraid—I'll live—even if—I'm supposed—to die."

Joe saying, "God will make that decision, Peggie."

"Oh—okay then—I can rest."

Shine. Shine.

"If you live, Peggie, Christ is with you here." Joe. "If you die, you will be with Christ there."

"Oh—silly me—if I live—God will love me. If I die—God

will—love me." Peg sinking into her pillows, into sleep.

Glory. Glory.

I taking advantage of Peg's sleep to empty out the drawer in her cabinet stuffed to overflowing with Lorna Doones and Oreos and RC Colas, not wanting the nurses to find her horde when they pack her things, perhaps think less of her.

John staring at Peg with incredulity for her extraordinary *If I live God will love me. If I die God will love me.* John staring at me with incredulity at my housekeeping, my doing the ordinary. "But, then, Mrs. Woodson, for your family maybe what Peggie said was ordinary."

John leaving at last. "We're so powerless, Reverend and Mrs. Woodson. This feeling is so awful. I have the same image running through my mind over and over. My sister told me about a guy she knew who worked at U.S. Steel. They have trains throughout the mill that carry—I don't know—ore or something, and this guy got caught on the track as a train was coming. Everyone was trying to pull him off the track. The trains move slowly, but they weigh hundreds of tons, so it takes miles to stop them. Everyone was pulling the man, screaming. The train crushed the man to death, slowly, while they all stood there powerless. . . ."

◊   ◊   ◊

Evening upon us.

Peg saying, "I'm afraid—I'm going—to die—because—I can't tell—God—it's okay—to be—an invalid. I know—He's not—a vindictive God—I know—He wouldn't—do that—to me—but it's easy—layin' here—to think—thoughts—like that."

Joe and I sitting, one on either side of her bed, each holding a hand. Peg sleeping before we can respond. Is she sleeping or in some state between sleeping and dying?

Joe and I huddling on my cot.

Peg waking, sitting up, a ghostly creature. I could whoosh my arm right through her. She summoning herself back from a far place, back to the graying woman and the balding man holding each other up on the cot beside her bed.

"You've been good," she says rhythmically, in a voice not her own, in words she has never used of us. "You've been good—moms and dads." The proclamation—her own.

She'd never say that if suddenly she were well again, Meg.

No, but she did say it, and no one can take it away from me.

"You've been good—moms and dads."

Oh, Peggie, epiphany.

Joe leaving for Ronald McDonald House, leaving me a beeper so I can reach him instantly.

Peggie unable to cough. Making bubbling sounds. Terrible sounds, but at least she is beyond coughing.

"I know Peg's life is being shortened, Jane, with her oxygen raised over and over. Her morphine increased."

"I couldn't be a doctor if I didn't do what I could to relieve human pain." Jane, the house doctor on duty through the night.

"We had a son once—Joey." I choking on my emotion. We did have a son once.

"He died nine years ago. At the end, when all hope was gone, we had to choose between raising his oxygen and letting him live comfortably for a day, or not raising his oxygen and letting him live in torment for a week. We chose the day. The choice has haunted me for nine years, but for nine years I've told myself I'd make the same choice for Peggie."

Jane hugging me, telling me it is a privilege to know me.

Why? We have just met. Yet I feel privileged to know her too.

Thank you, God, for all people who have a special knack for loving. Who say the right thing without trying. Jane, the burly stranger, Randy from Respiratory Therapy, the Domicron people, Lisa at Canterbury Manors. I would like to become one of these people, God.

Cousin Trude, on duty up the hall coming down and standing with me. "How are you doing, Mrs. Woodson?"

Everyone is kind. I wrapping myself up in my curtain and crying. I am so tired, and it is so dark.

◊   ◊   ◊

Joe's beeper going off. Something to do with a police car driving by, but Joe assuming the worst. "What is it, Meg? What?"

"Nothing, Joe. I didn't call." Midnight.

Joe's beeper going off three times in the midnight hours. "What, Meg? What?"

My panic mounting with each call. Something terrible must be happening. What? What?

Peg waking from the phone, talking rhythmically. "Read to me—from your handbook—Mother."

I, too tired to look beyond the cover, reading the cover. "Abandonment to Divine Providence."

"Oh, no—Mother—no, no." Voice of desolation. "Abandoned—abandoned—by God—"

"Oh, no, Peggie. Never abandoned by God, Peggie. We abandon ourselves to God, remember, like a baby in her father's arms?"

"Oh, right. I was scared—there—for a minute. Oh, *Ma—*"

"Peggie, when you see Joey, will you tell him that I love him?"

"I should tell—"

"Tell Joey that I still love him."

How many times have I told Joey that I still love him? But has he heard me? How many times have I asked God to tell Joey that I still love him? Asked God to send an angel to tell him? Yet having to send the message by his sister, by someone close to me in my world about to leave for his world.

"I should tell—Joseph—that—"

"That I still love him." Please, Peggie.

"I should tell—Joseph—that his mother—still loves—Joseph." Triumph.

My heart rocking my body, into bed, into sleep.

◊   ◊   ◊

"Mom, Mom." Peg calling.

211

I getting up, not knowing if I can. Going to her.

"Check the hall—check for movement—in the hall. Put out—the light. First—put out—the light. Check—for movement—in the hall."

I putting out the light, peeking cautiously out the door for movement in the hall.

"Get a pencil—get a pencil—get a paper." Peg talking rhythmically, in a voice not her own. "Write to John—write to John—under the covers—covers."

I stumbling back to bed. *I* will be dead by morning.

Peg calling, "Mom, Mom—come, come."

"What do you want, honey?"

"I don't—remember."

"If you need me, honey, I'll come. But if you don't need me, I'd better sleep."

"Okay—don't come—sleep—be happy."

I not coming. Sleeping.

Georgie coming. We have arranged for Georgie to check on Peggie every twenty minutes through the night. I can't have slept for twenty minutes.

Peggie saying, in a voice her own, not rhythmically, "I called—my mother—but my mother—wouldn't—help me."

Peggie, in touch with reality at one point only through this endless night, calling her mother—this dying daughter who will never call her mother again, and her mother would not help—her. *It is too much.*

How long did she lie there while I slept, hoping I would come? A lifetime? Yes. As long as it will take me to forgive myself for making her hope in vain. *It is too much.*

Georgie phoning Angie for Peg, as Angie has instructed should Peggie want to talk to her.

I not getting up, still not getting up, drifting off to sleep again, hearing Peg ramble to Angie about Jack the Ripper . . . the Boston Strangler. . . .

◊   ◊   ◊

I waking to silence. Only the dragging-in sounds of Peg's breathing breaking the ominous silence. I struggling up at last, going to Peggie.

212

Four A.M.

Peggie in a coma, beyond needing me.

I folding her limp hand in mine. It is so ugly, her hand. Her hands have always been ugly—coarse and stubby. It is so precious, her hand. She is more precious than all else in life to me.

I hearing the last thing she said to me. *Okay—don't come—sleep—be happy.* Knowing it is the last thing she will ever say to me, and that it echoes the accusations she has thrown at me throughout her lifetime . . . that I made her feel a burden . . . that I put my happiness before hers. As I often did.

I called—my mother—but my mother—wouldn't help me.

I cradling my cheek in her coarse, stubby hand and howling.

Nobody can hear. We are alone, my daughter and I, in a dimly lit alcove in an uninhabited land.

24

*I*nhuman screaming in the darkest hours, just before the dawn.

"Anyone you want to be here, get here." Jane.

"But—she's screamed before, Jane."

"She's convulsing now too, Mrs. Woodson."

"But—but—" No more buts.

Georgie calling Angie. I calling Joe. "She could die any minute, Joe."

I calling John. "This is the day, John." Monday.

Thursday, Friday, Saturday, Sunday . . . Monday. *Oh, God.*

Joe rushing in.

Angie rushing in.

The three of us attaching our eyes to Peggie as breath after faint breath keeps coming.

John not coming.

Eight o'clock. Angie calling John. "You're *what?* You're going to do *what?*" How like Peggie she sounds.

"He said he was going to work. He must be delirious, but *he is coming here now.*"

Jane, off-duty, but hovering near. "Who is Peggie waiting for?"

"John, her best friend." Angie.

"Sometimes, even when they're unconscious, they won't die till that one special person is present."

The Lerneys calling.

"Peggie is dying, Lou. You don't have time to get here."

I calm now. I must be calm.

Dr. Rathburn standing at the foot of Peg's bed. "Who is she waiting for?"

"John. She's waiting for her best friend, John."

Nine o'clock. Angie on the phone again. *"What?* You're afraid of *what?"*

"He's mumbling something about being a burden to you, Mrs. Woodson, but *he is on his way now."*

Georgie, long off-duty, wetting Peg's lips with a Q-tip.

Sandy, Peg's nurse for the day, sitting with us till the end. "I want you to know that it's time for Peg's medication, Mrs. Woodson. I'm not giving it to her, if that's all right with you, but I did want to mention that it's time."

I seeing why Peg worried that she might not die when she was supposed to. I not believing I am smiling.

John rushing in, a helter-skelter wind, fluttering over Peggie, settling down around Peggie as she lies on her deathbed covered with her pink butterfly sheet, mouth wide open in her old crone's face, hair stuck to her head in a black oily mat.

I glad for John's sake that he is here. Glad for my sake. For Peg's sake.

"It doesn't matter that she looks like that, does it, John?"

John outraged, but "No, it doesn't matter."

You're beautiful, Peggie. Yes, you are beautiful, and I love you dearly, more dearly than the spoken word can tell. . . . And I have loved you dearly, more dearly than the spoken word can tell.

The Lerneys rushing in, a wind that's been around. "Andy's here, Peggie. I don't know if you can hear me, but Andy and Lou and Lisa are here."

Lisa, the Lerney's oldest daughter who has been away at college, who hasn't seen Peggie since her happy wayfaring days, staring at her, mouth off-side in horror.

"If you were plotting a horror chart of C.F. deaths, Angie, where would you put Peg's death on the chart?"

216

"I've heard of one that was worse, but it was before my time."

Oh, Peggie. I want it over for you, Peggie.

The phone ringing. Sandy answering. "Who is this, please? . . . Jody? Mrs. Woodson can't come to the phone just now, Jody."

Jody, coming to the hospital that night, peering into fourth-floor rooms looking for Peggie.

"I'm going to ask Lisa to sit here on your cot, Mrs. Woodson." John. "Peggie won't look quite so bad to her from this angle."

I sitting on the left of Peg's bed in my mammoth blue robe. I knowing I will never forget this scene: Sandy sitting to my left at the head of the bed, titian hair shimmering about piquant face like the light of a setting sun, the tears on her cheeks wet stars; Lou sitting to my right; John and Angie and Lisa on the cot behind me; Angie in jeans, looking more like friend than nurse—which she is; Joe standing beside Peg on the right of her bed, and Andy standing next to him. Dr. Abinsky, our house doctor, at the foot of the bed, and beside her, Jane.

"Do you want to hold her, Mrs. Woodson?" Angie.

"No." I knowing Peggie Woodson would not want her mother to hold her. Peggie Woodson has done her own living, and Peggie Woodson will do her own dying. What if I tried to hold her and the slightest movement stopped her gossamer breaths? Peggie Woodson would die if her mother held her. . . .

And if she didn't. Peggie wisping out a tiniest-yet breath. All of us breathing in with her. All of us waiting. Angie running for Dr. Rathburn.

I, mind and heart and will as one, wisping *No, no no.* But her last breath wisping into the air. Gone.

Ten-fifty-five A.M. June 6. Margaret Ann Woodson. All gone.

My Peggie Woodson, all gone to me. *Oh, God. Oh, God.*

Pain jabbing John's whole body. The room crashing.

Joe breaking down, sobbing.

Then, pulling himself together, laying his hand on Peggie's soiled head. "I am the resurrection and the life," he quotes our Lord. "He that believeth in me, though he were dead, yet shall he live: And whosoever liveth and believeth in me shall never die." Joe's voice cracking, as it cracked when he spoke these words over Joey.

But then Joe speaking words for Peg alone: "Even though I walk through the valley of the shadow of death, I will fear no evil. . . . I go to prepare a place for you. . . . The Lord bless you and keep you: The Lord make his face to shine upon you, and be gracious unto to you: The Lord lift up his countenance upon you and give you peace."

All of us walking around Peg's bed, hugging each other. All of us who hold Peggie in our hearts holding each other in our arms and weeping.

I knowing that an endless pain has begun.

John and I walking down the hall to tell Liz that Peg has died. Mothers leaving their chairs beside the beds of their daughters and their sons, drifting into the hall, touching my arm, my hand as I pass.

I knowing I will not forget one touch.

Each of us from Peg's deathbed scene going in to her for a private good-bye.

I going to her last, walking as in a trance toward her. They've packed her things, dressed her in a clean hospital top. I don't know what weight. I touching her hand. It is still rough. It is still warm.

I turning from Peggie to the room. *What T-shirt shall I wear today, Mandy?* Where has the color gone? *420—gurgle-gurgle.* When did the dancing stop?

I knowing I cannot bear this pain.

I turning back to Peg, telling her again and again all the things I'm sorry I've done or haven't done in her lifetime, all the ways she's been a joy to me, how privileged I am to have had her. How proud I am that in her twenty-three years she's loved more than most of us who live three or four times twenty-three years. I making Peg a deathbed promise that I will go on a diet that very day and not go off it for as long as I live.

I wanting never to leave her. Never, never to rise from

this chair and walk away from her. But . . . they will come
and get me if I don't. Lead me out. But . . . *how can I leave
you alone here, Peggie?*

*Six weeks less one day, Peggie, since in the dawn's dove-
gray light, you set out on your fine, fierce, final odyssey. You
did it, Peggie. You laughed, and you loved, and you looked into
the face of God.*

*Oh, my Peggie. You turned your hardest of all times into
glory.*

25

Were you aware of your deathbed scene, Peggie? Oh, what a way to go.

And what about your arrival scene? Were Joey and New York Grandfather waiting for you? Did Jesus hug you? What did Joey say when you gave him my message? Does he still love me?

We had your funeral in the church. All your friends from ninth grade Advanced English came except one who was sick and one who was in California, and your college friends came from all over creation. There was such a traffic jam in the street, we had to delay the start of the service, and the deacons declared the crowd the biggest ever in the Church in the Woods. You were popular that day, Peggie.

John and Angie sat with us in the family pew. Liz took a leave of absence from the hospital to come. Her mother drove her.

Andy Lerney talked about what a brilliant student you were, and Becky's mother told about the time you went on a trip with them and their little car rammed into a truck full of pigs, and she wanted to brain you because you were so excited to be having such a big adventure. And Jacqui said that you were the person who taught her how to love.

Shelley met me at the door of the church with a big yellow smiley-face mum, and I got up holding the mum and talked about Edith Schaeffer's saying, "There's a Peggie

*Woodson inside your body that wants to get out and can't,"
and how you said that you did want to get out of your body,
and how now you were out, your health and happiness beyond our ability to imagine.*

*I've pondered, Peggie, why, when I made you a deathbed
promise, I promised to do something that was important to
me rather than to you. At first I put it down to selfishness,
but more and more I realize that I made you that promise
because I knew, under all my doubting, that what was important to me was important to you because I was important
to you. I promised you I would go on a diet because I knew
you loved me.*

*You do know, don't you, Peggie, beyond all doubting,
that I always have and always will love you?*

*Your father will be lonely for you until he sees you
again—sometimes he can hardly wait.*

*He befriended a little girl in our church after you died.
Joelle needed a man in her life, and your father needed a
girl-child in his. Joelle means a lot to us both.*

*I did get my counseling degree, Peg, and have a small
private practice now, though I spend more of my time writing.*

*John is married. If you'd had approval right over his
choice of a wife, you'd have approved, no question. John
asked your father and me to sit with his family at the wedding, and Angie came home and sat with us and Lester and
his wife at the reception.*

*Did you know they discovered the C.F. gene last year?
And just yesterday it was on the news that they injected
the faulty C.F. gene with a healthy one, and the faulty one
became healthy. Of course that's in a test tube, but they're
expecting a breakthrough. . . . It's so wonderful, but it's hard
for me to think about too.*

*So, what's new with you, Peggie? What glorious adven-
tures are you up to now?*